# GLADYS GETS GRILLED.

"IT'S REALLY NOT THAT HARD if you just follow a recipe!" Gladys exclaimed. "And if you let me teach you both some basic knife skills, we can—"

"Whoa, whoa, whoa," her mom said. "You will not be doing *anything* with knives. In fact, if any cooking happens—and I'm not saying it will—then you'll have no part in it. Understood?"

Gladys didn't want to agree, but she didn't seem to have any other options. "Okay," she mumbled. *But,* she added in her head, *there's no way I'm eating only your awful food for six whole months*. Her parents might be able to ban her from the kitchen, but they couldn't stop her from cooking up some kind of survival plan.

"Good, that's settled," her dad said, pushing himself up from the sofa. "Now, let's go nuke some of that pizza. I'm starving!"

Gladys made a mental note to aim for the microwave the next time she set the kitchen on fire.

## OTHER BOOKS YOU MAY ENJOY

# ALL FOUR
# STARS

Tara Dairman

**PUFFIN BOOKS**
An Imprint of Penguin Group (USA)

★ ★ ★ ★

PUFFIN BOOKS
Published by the Penguin Group
Penguin Group (USA) LLC
375 Hudson Street
New York, New York 10014

USA * Canada * UK * Ireland * Australia
New Zealand * India * South Africa * China

penguin.com
A Penguin Random House Company

First published in the United States of America by G. P. Putnam's Sons,
an imprint of Penguin Young Readers Group, 2014
Published by Puffin Books, an imprint of Penguin Young Readers Group, 2015

THE LIBRARY OF CONGRESS HAS CATALOGED THE G. P. PUTNAM'S SONS EDITION AS FOLLOWS:
Dairman, Tara.
All four stars / Tara Dairman.
pages cm
Summary: Eleven-year-old Gladys Gatsby loves food and cooking, so when
she lands an assignment to write a restaurant review for a New York City
newspaper, she will do anything to make it happen, even risk the wrath of her
fast-food-loving parents.
ISBN 978-0-399-16252-7 (hc)
[1. Cooking—Fiction. 2 Family life—New York—Fiction. 3. Schools—Fiction.
4. Journalism—Fiction. 5. Friendship—Fiction. 6. New York (State)—Fiction.]
I. Title.   PZ7.D1521127All 2014   [Fic]—dc23   2013026297

Puffin Books ISBN 978-0-14-242636-4

Printed in the United States of America

13 15 17 19 20 18 16 14 12

*For Katie, Jess, Evelyn, and Miriam*

# Chapter 1

# A GREAT, BIG, FAT AMOUNT OF TROUBLE

GLADYS GATSBY STOOD AT THE COUNTER with the spout of her father's heavy blowtorch poised over the ceramic cup. Her finger hovered over the trigger button that was supposed to turn her plain little custards into crunchy, tasty treats. That's when she heard a car door slam outside.

She froze for a second, but then checked the clock. It was 5:16—still a good forty-four minutes before her parents were due home from work, and they were never early. *It's probably just the neighbors,* she told herself, and turned back to her project.

Gladys knew her torch wasn't the right kind for making desserts—it was a

★ ★ ★ ★

lot bigger than the one pictured in her cookbook, for starters, plus there was that huge DANGER: EXTREMELY FLAMMABLE label on its side. But she never abandoned a cooking experiment just because her parents didn't have the right kitchen equipment. Just last week she'd rolled out pie dough with the stick of a broken umbrella, and it had turned out great.

*Still,* she thought as she repositioned the torch's nozzle, *it would've been nice if they'd given me the minitorch I wanted for my eleventh birthday instead of that stupid tablet computer.*

But they hadn't, so she was stuck with this old clunker from the garage. *Oh well,* she thought, and crossing her toes for luck inside her sneakers (her hands were kind of full), she took a deep breath and pulled the trigger.

Several things happened at once.

With a pop, a blue flame quite a few inches longer than she'd expected shot out of the blowtorch, passing clear over the far edge of the first custard cup.

With a whoosh, the wintery wind outside changed direction and began to blow in through the kitchen window, setting the gauzy blue-and-white curtains aflutter.

And with a jingle and a grinding noise and finally a click, someone turned a key in the Gatsbys' front door.

A moment later, she heard her parents' footsteps in the hall.

"Gladdy!" her dad called. "We've got pizza!"

*Fudge!* Gladys thought. She tried to release the trigger on the blowtorch, but to her horror, the spout kept shooting flame. She pumped it desperately with her finger, but that only seemed to make the flame bigger.

Their footsteps were getting louder.

Gripping the torch firmly, Gladys did her best to direct the now-enormous flame off the countertop and back over her cluster of custards. The tops turned brown from the heat almost immediately. She pumped the trigger again and, miraculously, this time heard a click as it released against her finger. The long blue flame started to retreat back into the torch's nozzle.

But then, at the exact moment her mom and dad stepped into the kitchen—the exact moment that Gladys was about to spin around and explain that she had the situation perfectly under control—the fluttering kitchen curtains crossed paths with the dying blowtorch flame and promptly caught on fire.

The flames couldn't have traveled up the blue-and-white fabric faster if it had been soaked in gasoline. Gladys staggered backward, and in an instant her whole secret cooking life flashed before her eyes.

She saw herself as a little kid, playing chef by

mixing things in the giant ceramic bowl her parents had received as a housewarming present and never used.

She saw herself reading her first cookbook at the age of eight, and riding home from her first solo trip to Mr. Eng's Gourmet Grocery, her bike basket stuffed with ingredients for pasta primavera.

Nine. Ten. Eleven. She saw herself stewing tomatoes and steaming mussels, tossing spring salads and grilling steaks, rolling her own sushi and whipping her own whipped cream. She saw herself opening windows to air out the smell of her cooking and taking out trash bags full of eggshells and vegetable peels. She saw herself stashing leftovers in the rusty old fridge in the garage that no one else used anymore judging from the contents (two dented soda cans and a dried-up tube of superglue).

It was during one of those garage trips that she had first noticed the blowtorch, neglected in the corner . . .

The sound of the smoke alarm shocked Gladys back to the present. Her dad's briefcase clattered to the floor as he grabbed her arm and dragged her away from the window. Her mom's hair flew out of its bun as she ripped the fire extinguisher from the wall. White powder filled the air all around them as she sprayed the kitchen, and Gladys knew one thing for sure: Today would *not* be remembered as the day she proved what a great cook she was and earned more kitchen privileges. No, today would forever be the day Gladys Gatsby set the house on fire . . . and, if her family survived, the day she got into a great, big, fat amount of trouble.

# Chapter 2

## GLADYS GETS GRILLED

TEN MINUTES LATER, GLADYS SAT ON the living room sofa, staring down at her sneakers. They'd been tomato red earlier, but were now more of a salmon color, thanks to the white extinguisher powder smudged across the canvas.

Gladys didn't normally get into trouble, so she didn't know a lot about punishments other than what she'd read in books. Would she be grounded? Assigned to do backbreaking chores? Forced to live in a cupboard under the stairs?

She snuck a glance at her parents, who stood a few feet away, talking quietly. Her mom's stockings were ripped, and wisps of her dark brown hair stuck out at crazy

★ ★ ★ ★

angles. Her dad's glasses balanced awkwardly on his beaky nose, and a streak of soot darkened one arm of his dress shirt. Neither of them looked very happy.

Not wanting to catch their attention, Gladys quickly shifted her gaze to the Christmas tree in the corner. Its lights blinked on and off, illuminating the ornaments her aunt Lydia had sent her over the years. Her favorite one—a hot pepper with her name engraved on it—blazed to life, then fell back into darkness.

"Gladdy?"

Gladys jumped. Her stomach began to churn queasily, like it did after eating the greasy takeout her parents brought home most nights from Sticky Burger or Fred's Fried Fowl.

"Yes?" she said as bravely as she could.

Her father knelt down beside the sofa. "Let's start at the beginning," he said. "Can you explain to us what, exactly, you were doing in the kitchen?"

Gladys told the truth. "I was making crème brûlée."

"Crumb broo-lay?" Gladys's dad looked up at his wife quizzically, but she just shrugged. "What is crumb broo-lay?"

Gladys sighed. If a dish wasn't on the menu at one of the fast-food joints in town, her parents didn't know it existed. "It's a dessert," she explained. "A custard with a crust of burnt sugar on top. *Brûlée* means *burnt* in French."

"So now we have curtains brûlée, huh?" Gladys's dad laughed at his little joke. But her mom didn't seem to think it was funny as she stepped forward to take over the interrogation. She had white extinguisher powder on her face, and her red lipstick was smeared. The combination made her look like a clown—a scary clown.

"Gladys," Clown-Mom said, moving her hands to her hips, "who taught you how to make this crumb . . . thing?"

Gladys took a deep breath. "I taught myself," she said. "I've seen chefs do it on TV, and I found the recipe in one of my cookbooks, so—"

"So you thought you'd just drag your father's blowtorch out of the garage and take a crack at it?"

"No!" Gladys cried. "I mean, I didn't just . . . decide to do it and go get the blowtorch. I planned it really carefully. Normally I'm a very good cook."

"Normally?" Her mom raised one powder-dusted eyebrow.

Uh-oh.

Gladys's dad jumped back in. "Gladdy," he said, "is this the first time you've been cooking on your own?"

The churning sensation in Gladys's stomach gave way to a sinking one as she shook her head.

"But why didn't you let us help?" her dad said. "We could have cooked this crumb thing together."

Gladys thought back to the few times she *had* tried to cook with her parents. It had always been a disaster.

If Gladys let her mom buy the supplies for a recipe, she would come home with the low-fat and sugar-free versions of every ingredient, insisting that they tasted the same as the regular ones.

They didn't.

But at least she looked at the recipe. Gladys's dad didn't believe in recipes, so if Gladys left him alone for even one minute, he'd start throwing in random stuff, saying that experimenting always made a dish taste better.

It didn't.

Worst of all, even if they managed to cobble together a decent mixture of ingredients, Gladys's parents refused to use the oven or the stovetop—not when they could just nuke things in the microwave.

"You can't bake cookies in a microwave!" Gladys had cried during their last, most catastrophic family cooking project. "It says right here: 'Bake for eight to ten minutes at 350 degrees *in the oven*'!"

"Oh, it all works the same way," her mom had said as Gladys's dad scooped spoonfuls of dough directly onto the glass carousel.

Why did Gladys even bother? It wasn't like the cookies could have been saved at that point anyway.

They were already full of light margarine instead of butter, zero-calorie sweetener instead of sugar, and four times as much baking soda as the recipe called for, which her dad said would make them "extra light and fluffy."

So when the cookies had swelled to the size of grapefruits and exploded, Gladys wasn't surprised. But her parents were baffled.

"See, this is why I hate to cook," her mom had complained as she scraped burnt dough off the inside of the microwave door. "You put in all this effort, and it never comes out right!"

That had been almost a year ago, and since then Gladys had only dared to cook while her parents were at work.

But now her father was looking at her curiously, waiting to find out why she never asked them for help. Gladys couldn't tell him to his face that they were terrible cooks—not after what she'd just done to the kitchen.

"Well, you guys never really seem to . . . *enjoy* cooking," Gladys said carefully. "So I thought that it would be better for everyone if I just did it on my own."

"And burned down the house in the process?" her mom snapped.

"That was just an accident!" Gladys knew her parents had a right to be upset, but she also felt like they were the ones who had forced her to do all the sneaking around in the first place. Now, like a forgotten pot heating on the back burner, her anger was boiling over. "I've made 142 other recipes from twelve different cookbooks," she cried, "and they all turned out fine!"

Gladys could tell as it was coming out of her mouth that this was the wrong thing to say, but she couldn't stop herself. Now both of her parents were staring at her like she was an alien.

"Did you say one hundred . . . and forty . . . two?" her dad gasped.

An alien who cooked. A lot.

Gladys's dad's eyes were now as round as the measuring cups he never used, and her mom actually stood up and backed a step away from her, as if her cooking disease might be contagious.

"How—how did you do this?" she stuttered. "*When* did you do this?"

"I just messed around after school sometimes," Gladys said, trying too late to sound like it was no big deal. "And during vacations, I guess." It was winter break now, and so far Gladys had taken advantage of every minute her parents spent at work. She'd memorized their schedules, making sure to scour the kitchen and sneak her leftovers out to the garage fridge well before they got home each day. If only they hadn't chosen tonight to leave their offices early and surprise her.

Gladys's mom was pacing the room. "You know, we've tried to support your interests, Gladys," she said, her voice rising. "We gave you cookbooks, which you promised were just for reading. We subscribed to that Planet Food channel, which you promised was just for watching. We've even tried to organize family cooking projects from time to time . . . and this is how you repay us? By putting yourself in danger behind our backs?"

She sank into the cushion next to Gladys on the sofa and placed a hand on her daughter's shoulder. "It's just that, well . . . we worry about you, honey," she said in a softer voice. "When I was your age, I was on the swim team, and your dad played basketball, and we both had lots of friends. But you only seem to want to stay home and"—she glanced in the direction of the kitchen—"cook, I guess. What about making friends? What about having fun?"

"Cooking *is* fun . . ." Gladys started, but her dad shook his head.

"Your mom's right," he said, "and we're going to have to set some new rules around here. First of all, your allowance is suspended until the fire damage is all paid off."

Gladys nodded. That seemed fair.

"And we think that it's time for you to explore some new hobbies. So, I'm sorry, but the cooking is going to have to stop."

"S-stop?" Gladys wasn't sure what her father was saying.

"Yes," her mom agreed. "No more cooking, no more cookbooks, and no more cooking TV shows for the next six months."

*"Six months?!"* Gladys couldn't believe it. That took her right up to the end of sixth grade. What was she supposed to do every day after school?

Her mom seemed to read her mind. "So after Christmas," she said, "you can start doing some more . . . *normal* activities for a kid your age. You can hang out with other kids—"

"But—"

"And play more computer games—"

"But—"

"And . . . go to the mall!"

"Why would I want to go to the mall?"

"Gladdy, we're serious," her dad said, and the grim expression on his face meant that he was telling the truth.

"Well, what am I supposed to *eat?*" Gladys asked.

Her parents exchanged a confused look. "What do you mean?" her mom asked. "You'll eat what we always eat."

Gladys thought of the bland, floppy vegetables her parents brought home from Palace of Wong, the falling-apart sandwiches they got at Sticky Burger, and the goopy, undercooked crusts of the pizzas from Pathetti's Pies.

"But the food we eat is gross," she said. "It tastes awful and makes me feel sick. That's why I like to cook my own food."

The room was uncomfortably silent for a moment, then Gladys's dad cleared his throat. "Well, maybe your mom and I will try to cook more often," he said.

"You will?" Gladys gasped.

"We will?" her mom gasped.

Gladys's dad turned to his wife. "Look, if an eleven-year-old can do it, how hard can it be?"

"It's really not that hard if you just follow a recipe!" Gladys exclaimed. "And if you let me teach you both some basic knife skills, we can—"

"Whoa, whoa, whoa," her mom said. "You will not be doing *anything* with knives. In fact, if any cooking happens—and I'm not saying it will—then you'll have no part in it. Understood?"

Gladys didn't want to agree, but she didn't seem to have any other options. "Okay," she mumbled. *But,* she added in her head, *there's no way I'm eating only your awful food for six whole months.* Her parents might be able to ban her from the kitchen, but they couldn't stop her from cooking up some kind of survival plan.

"Good, that's settled," her dad said, pushing

himself up from the sofa. "Now, let's go nuke some of that pizza. I'm starving!"

Gladys made a mental note to aim for the micro-wave the next time she set the kitchen on fire.

# Chapter 3

# THE SECRET COOKBOOK

GLADYS TOSSED AND TURNED SO MUCH in bed that night that the half-raw pizza dough in her stomach probably got flipped a hundred times. The harder she tried to fall asleep, the more she thought about the events of the day—and the years of cooking that had led up to it.

It had all started with a visit from her aunt Lydia.

Aunt Lydia was Gladys's mom's sister, but the two were as different as mushrooms and milk shakes. Aunt Lydia lived in Paris, while Gladys's mom hated big cities. Aunt Lydia's trunks burst with colorful scarves, while Gladys's mom's closet held row after row of dark business suits. But most importantly, Aunt Lydia

★ ★ ★ ★

loved great food, while Gladys's mom—and dad—felt exactly the opposite.

The summer when Gladys turned seven, Aunt Lydia had visited from France. Every day she and Gladys took walks together around East Dumpsford, the Long Island suburb where the Gatsbys lived.

"This town is nothing like Paris," Aunt Lydia sniffed as they made their way down the main street one day. "All the houses here look the same, and instead of a lovely Eiffel Tower, you have that stinky landfill. But maybe things will look prettier to us if we eat something good while we explore."

Indeed, Aunt Lydia's mood often seemed to improve when she was eating—and she always had some kind of strange, delicious snack in her purse. On any given day she might offer her niece a dried persimmon dipped in chocolate, a lavender-flavored sandwich cookie, or a pretzel coated with a green powder called wasabi that made Gladys's eyes water. But Gladys loved the weird snacks, and as they walked through town she tried to point out more places where her aunt could find food.

"That's where we get dinner on Mondays," she told her as they strolled past the Pathetti's sign, with its flashing pizza pies inside each giant *P.* "And we eat Fred's on Tuesdays." She pointed up at the glowing chicken bucket that rotated outside of Fred's Fried Fowl. "And Wednesday night is Sticky's night!" she said as they passed under the huge plastic hamburger that dripped neon pink sauce high above the Sticky Burger drive-thru. "Do you eat at restaurants a lot in Paris?"

"Oh, Gladys!" Aunt Lydia burst out. Her scarves flapped in the breeze as she pulled her niece around to face her. "Those are *not* restaurants," she said, pointing back at the strip of fast-food joints with a shiver of disgust. But then, slowly, a smile spread across her wasabi-dusted lips. "How would you like to see what a *real* restaurant looks like?"

Fifteen minutes later, they were at the East Dumpsford train station, Aunt Lydia punching buttons on a machine to buy them two tickets to New York City. The city was only an hour away, and Gladys's dad took the train there and back every day for work, but Gladys had never been. She clutched her aunt's hand tightly as they boarded the silver train, then she watched as Middle Dumpsford, West Dumpsford, and Far Dumpsford whipped by outside her window. Eventually the train dipped into a dark tunnel, and then all at once they were pulling into Penn Station in the heart of Manhattan.

"I did a little college here before I moved to France, you know," Aunt Lydia told Gladys as they rode the enormous escalator up to the street, "and I bet I can still remember all the best places to eat!"

Their first destination was an Ethiopian restaurant on Tenth Avenue, where the tables looked like colorful baskets and wailing songs played over the speaker system. Their food came out on a huge round plate, and instead of using forks or spoons, they scooped spicy bites of pureed beans and chunks of meaty stew into their mouths using their fingers and a spongy bread called injera. Gladys had never eaten anything like it.

Next, Aunt Lydia took Gladys on the subway to a crowded kosher restaurant on the Lower East Side. There they shared a table with a pair of bushy-bearded men and slurped chicken soup from steaming bowls. Gladys's favorite part was the giant spongy ball—a matzo ball, her aunt called it—that bobbed up and down in her broth.

After walking around a bit more, they finally rode a bus to Chinatown, where they sat on duct-taped chairs in the window of a tiny eatery and feasted on dumplings filled with tender pork and crunchy scallions. Gladys didn't understand how the dough surrounding the dumplings could feel both soft and crispy in her mouth at the same time, but that didn't stop her from finishing an entire plate.

"Now *that*," said Aunt Lydia each time she led a full-tummied Gladys back out onto the bustling streets of Manhattan, "was a restaurant!"

And Gladys had to agree. The food she was eating with her aunt tasted nothing like what her parents picked up for dinner in East Dumpsford. She wasn't sure she could ever enjoy a Sticky Burger again.

Walking home from the train station that night, Gladys asked her aunt how the cooks in New York City got their food to taste so good.

"Is it magic?" she wondered out loud.

Aunt Lydia let out a throaty laugh. "No, my sweet Gladiola," she said, using one of the flowery nicknames she'd given her niece. "I suppose it's part science and part art." Then she explained as best she could how the right amount of heat, for the right amount of time, combined with just the right amount of this spice or that sauce, could make the right ingredients taste incredible.

"I wish that I could teach you more about cooking," she continued as they turned into the Gatsbys' driveway, "but your parents seem dead set against my using the kitchen at all. And while I'm a guest in their house, I don't want to break their rules."

So instead of cooking, Aunt Lydia and Gladys continued with their walks around East Dumpsford. One day, near the end of the summer, they came upon a dusty-looking shop that they had never noticed before.

"Mr. Eng's Gourmet Grocery," Aunt Lydia read from the faded sign in the window. "Well, shall we have a look?" Gladys nodded, and her aunt pushed open the

rickety wooden door. A little bell chimed overhead—
and suddenly, they were in a different world.

The aroma from the wall of spices hit Gladys first,
tickling her nose with sharp, exotic scents she had
never smelled before. To her left stood a refrigerator
full of cheeses: wheels and wedges in shades of red
and yellow and blue. And toward the back of the store
there were piles of purple potatoes, yellow tomatoes,
and orange peppers; a bin full of tiny, spiny pink
fruits; and a stack of great green squashes with necks
curved like swans.

"My goodness," Aunt Lydia murmured. "I didn't
think that a place like this could exist in East Dumpsford!" With every word she spoke, she inched closer to
the cheese refrigerator, as if she were a magnet that
belonged on its door.

Gladys wandered over to the spice wall and picked
up a jar filled with little striped seeds. CUMIN, the label
said. She gave the jar a shake, and the seeds responded
with a satisfying, maraca-like rattle.

"Would you like to try some?"

Gladys whirled around and found herself staring
up at a tall, slender man with bushy eyebrows and
inky-black hair shot with gray. His eyes were kind behind his wire-rimmed glasses, crinkling in the corners
as he smiled down at her.

"I haven't seen you in here before. I'm Mr. Eng,
of course." As he spoke, the man reached down and

gently took the jar of cumin out of Gladys's hands. Then, motioning for her to hold out her palm, he unscrewed the top and tapped a few seeds onto it. As she crunched on them, she found that they tasted rich like nuts, sharp like licorice, and even a little bit fiery.

"Do you have a spice grinder at home?" Mr. Eng asked.

Gladys shook her head no.

"Well, we'd better start with something more basic than cumin, then." His eyes roved over the hundreds of glass jars stacked up against the wall. "Here," he said, pulling down a jar of red-brown powder. The label said EXTRA-FANCY VIETNAMESE CINNAMON. "It's already ground, so you don't have to do a thing but sprinkle it on top of any sweet dish. Pancakes, oatmeal, and of course cakes and pies. Let's go get you a bag." His long legs carried him swiftly toward the checkout counter, and Gladys scurried after him.

"But I don't have any money," she said.

Mr. Eng chuckled softly. "Haven't you ever heard of free samples?" He pulled a small plastic bag out of a drawer behind the counter and scooped some cinnamon into it. "This one's on the house."

And so Gladys went home that day with her first ingredient. If it wasn't for Aunt Lydia, she probably would have just tucked the bag away in a drawer, letting it make her pajamas smell nice. But instead, she couldn't stop thinking about cooking with it. Could she use the cinnamon—or other spices from the wall at Mr. Eng's—to recreate the kinds of foods she and her aunt had eaten together in the city? If so, how?

The answer came in the mail a few weeks after Aunt Lydia's return to Paris.

At first glance, the package appeared to contain a famous children's book: the one with the Eiffel Tower and two straight lines of girls on the cover. But when Gladys peeked inside, she saw that the jacket had been swapped.

It was a cookbook.

Then, deeper in the package she found a smaller book with blank pages and an inscription inside the cover. *Here is a journal for recording all of the lovely things you eat and cook,* it said in tiny letters. *The cooking can be our secret.*

And Gladys had kept that secret—until today.

# Chapter 4

# A FOODIE GROUP OF ONE

CHRISTMAS DINNER A FEW DAYS LATER was its usual sad affair. Gladys's parents took her to the Happy Rainbow All-U-Can-Eat Buffet—which Gladys had always thought was a funny name, since the foods they served only came in one color. But as she picked over this year's plate of dry brown turkey, sticky brown stuffing, and soupy brown "green" beans, she didn't think she would ever be able to laugh about food again.

Gladys wrote in her journal as soon as she got home.

*Another Christmas at the big brown buffet. The food this year seemed even browner than usual. Maybe the*

★ ★ ★ ★

*new heat lamps they got are stronger, like those tanning beds people lie in when they want to pretend they just went on a tropical vacation? The turkey definitely looked like it had spent some time on a desert island—and tasted like it, too.*

*Anyway, this year's award for the most impressively brown thing that should never be brown has to go to the Jell-O. I wonder what flavor it was supposed to be. Nutmeg? Root beer? Beef? I took a tiny bite off Dad's plate, and I'm still not sure.*

*The sad thing is that there are so many nice brown foods—like soy sauce, and dark chocolate, and fresh-baked whole wheat bread. Why can't the buffet serve any of those?*

★↲ *(food edible, but nowhere near delicious)*

Gladys closed her journal gently. It wasn't the original one Aunt Lydia had sent—that book had filled up years ago—but since then her aunt had made sure to slip a new one into Gladys's birthday package each year. The latest had a simple red leather cover, and Gladys always felt better after reviewing her meals in it. She used a four-star rating system, just like the critics at the *New York Standard* newspaper did, though she'd never had a meal that earned all four stars. Still, Gladys was always hopeful that an amazing four-star meal might be right around the corner. She even carried the journal with her at school, just in case a swapped-for lunch surprised her—and because scribbling down reviews gave her something to do while everybody else was off playing at recess.

Gladys wasn't looking forward to going back to school next week. She'd had plenty of friends when she was younger—it seemed like everyone was friends back then, or at least all the girls were. Everyone got invited to everyone else's birthday parties, and if Gladys examined her piece of birthday cake a little too critically before eating it, no one seemed to care.

But last year, in fifth grade, everything had changed. Or maybe it happened the summer before at Camp Bentley, where most of the kids in town went. All Gladys knew was that when she got back to school that year, everyone seemed to be part of a group. And whether it was the soccer players, or the brainiacs, or the super-popular girls, every group seemed to be on guard against anyone who was too weird or different. Suddenly, one random comment about a delicious arugula salad could get you laughed at for weeks. Gladys was alone, in a foodie group of one.

Now, as she tucked her journal back into its hiding place under the bed, Gladys thanked her lucky star fruits that her parents didn't know she was writing about food. If they did, they probably would have banned that for the next six months, too.

At home the morning of her first day back at school, Gladys was daydreaming about pho bo—the Vietnamese beef- and noodle-filled breakfast soup that she had cooked once in fourth grade—when she heard a horn honk outside. She looked out the window to see Sandy Anderson dashing out of his house next door, his blond hair flattened down with gel. He had a backpack over one shoulder and his school blazer flung over the other.

Sandy was a year younger than Gladys and had gone to a private school ever since he and his mother had moved in last year. The day after the Andersons arrived, Sandy's mom had sent him over to introduce himself and ask if he could borrow a cup of sugar. He quietly mumbled that she wanted to bake cupcakes but wasn't finished unpacking all of their kitchen supplies. Of course, the Gatsbys didn't have any sugar. But, trying her best to be neighborly, Gladys's mom sent him home with a handful of pastel-colored packets of artificial sweetener that she found in a box next to the instant coffee.

Gladys observed the whole exchange from the top of the stairs, then moved to the window to watch Sandy hurry home. A minute after he disappeared into his house, the Andersons' front door opened again and an annoyed-looking Mrs. Anderson rushed out to her car and drove away, probably to buy some real sugar. Sandy had not been back to the Gatsbys' house since.

Now, Gladys watched Sandy's bus disappear down the block.

"You've hardly touched your cereal!" her mom cried, snapping Gladys's attention back to the food in front of her.

*"Mom,"* Gladys said, shoving the bowl of fake apple–flavored rings across the table, "the milk is *green*."

They compromised on an energy bar, which Gladys ate in the car. She usually just rode the few blocks to school on her bicycle, but her mom insisted on driving today. "It's too cold outside to ride on that bike," she said, but Gladys suspected that her mom's real motive was to keep her from stopping at Mr. Eng's on the way to or from school.

It was too bad, since visiting Mr. Eng was usually the highlight of Gladys's day. She liked to alphabetize his canned tomato products (crushed, diced, paste, pureed, stewed, whole) as she munched on a fresh clementine from the fruit bin (and, okay, maybe a jam-filled croissant from the pastry case). Plus there was Mr. Eng himself, who always had time to tell Gladys about his latest gourmet imports. He was good at listening, too; if she'd stopped there this morning, Gladys surely would have told him that she was nervous—but also excited—about getting a new teacher.

Mrs. Wellchurch had left in December to have a baby, though Gladys wasn't sad to see her go. She had known that she was in for a long, boring year after their first assignment. Mrs. Wellchurch had forced everyone to read their "How I Spent My Summer Vacation" essays out loud, and Gladys didn't know which was worse, having to share that she spent the summer at home with a babysitter, or having to hear about what all the other kids did at Camp Bentley, the camp run by Charissa Bentley's parents. Charissa was the prettiest—but also the meanest—girl in Gladys's grade, and Gladys refused to spend any more time with her than she already had to during the school year.

As her mom turned the car into the school parking lot, a horrible thought struck Gladys. What if their new teacher made them all write about what they'd done over winter break? Gladys doubted that an essay called "How I Stole My Dad's Blowtorch and Set the Kitchen on Fire" would make the best first impression (even if it would make her temporarily more popular among some of the pyromaniac boys).

"I'll pick you up right here at three o'clock," Gladys's mom said as she pulled up in front of the school. "I'm sure you'll be anxious to catch up with the other kids, but try to be out here on time so I can get back to the office, okay?"

Gladys nodded blankly and shut the car door behind her. If she needed any more proof that her mom was completely clueless about her life at school, this was it.

## Chapter 5

# A TASTE OF THE FUTURE

TRUE TO GLADYS'S SUSPICIONS, NO one bothered to say hello to her as she made her way through the front entrance of East Dumpsford Elementary. But when she walked into classroom 116 a minute later, total mayhem greeted her.

Several desks were pushed out of their neat rows. Jake Wheeler had apparently stolen Owen Green's snow boot, and Owen was hopping around and swiping at Jake, trying to get it back. Three other kids were standing at the blackboard, drawing funny faces with chalk. And in the middle of the classroom, sitting haughtily on top of a desk and surveying her surroundings, was Charissa Bentley.

★ ★ ★ ★

Deeply tanned from her Caribbean vacation, sporting designer jeans and a purple top, and with her shiny brown hair gathered up into a very high ponytail, Charissa looked around as if she owned the place. When she saw Gladys in the doorway, she shouted, "Gladys Gatsby!" for everyone to hear.

Gladys's heart thudded like a lump of dough being slapped onto a countertop. She heard giggles and noticed that to Charissa's left and right sat her two best friends, Rolanda Royce and Marti Astin. They were also wearing jeans and purple shirts, and except for Rolanda's tiny black braids and Marti's wild orange curls, they looked like Charissa clones.

Gladys was usually far beneath the notice of the most popular girl in her grade, but if Charissa had decided to pick on her, Gladys might as well turn around and ask to be homeschooled. Charissa could make anyone she chose miserable. What would she make fun of first? Gladys's pageboy haircut? Her super-pale skin? The new lobster backpack Aunt Lydia had sent this Christmas? (It had seemed like a cool present when Gladys took it out of the box, but now she wasn't so sure.) Charissa opened her pink lip gloss–stained mouth again to speak, and Gladys braced for an insult—but was surprised to hear the words "Jesse Wall!" come out instead.

Gladys turned around and almost smacked right

into Jesse, a skinny boy with glasses who was coming through the doorway behind her. So Charissa wasn't picking on anybody yet—she had simply taken it upon herself to announce everyone's arrivals. That was a very Charissa-like thing to do, since she liked to be in charge. Relieved, Gladys hurried to her desk and took a seat, and she saw Jesse (a little pink around the ears at having his entrance announced) do the same. A moment later, everyone else was scurrying for their seats when the new teacher entered.

The teacher turned out to be a tall woman with skin the color of a walnut shell and short, licorice-black hair. She wore a straight purple skirt that came down to her knees, a green blouse, and brown boots that reached halfway up her legs. A thick string of turquoise beads hung around her neck, as did a pair of red-framed eyeglasses on a string. Gladys couldn't help but think she looked a little ridiculous.

"Good morning," the teacher said crisply, setting a leopard-print briefcase down on her desk. If she heard the giggles from Charissa and her cronies, she ignored them. "My name is Ms. Quincy. Please take your seats." She placed the red glasses on her nose and peered around the room until her eyes came to rest on Charissa, Rolanda, and Marti. "Rest assured, however, that if I find you talking to your neighbors during lessons, you *will* be moved."

Charissa scowled. Gladys liked Ms. Quincy already.

"Now," Ms. Quincy continued, "I am aware that some teachers like to start the term off by having their students write about what they did during their vacations." She paused and picked up a piece of chalk. "But I think that is an idiotic assignment."

Gladys's heart nearly leapt for joy.

"Instead," Ms. Quincy went on, "I would like our first assignment together to be something more meaningful. You will all be writing stories about your futures, which I imagine—which I *hope*—will be much more interesting than anything that happened to you over the last two weeks."

Ms. Quincy turned to the board and wrote the word *Future*. Gladys heard a muffled noise and turned to see Charissa whispering to Rolanda. A moment later, Rolanda's hand was waving frantically in the air.

"Yes?" said the teacher, laying her chalk back down in its tray.

"But Ms. Quincy," Rolanda cried breathlessly, "how can we write about the future when we don't know what's going to *happen*?"

"Aha," replied Ms. Quincy. "That is where your imagination comes in. With a little creativity, anything is possible. It will be up to you to figure out what your future may hold."

Charissa looked unhappy. Unless it was coming up

with new insults, creativity was not her strong suit. Gladys's brain, meanwhile, was immediately buzzing with thoughts of all the delicious meals her future might bring.

"The most exciting news," Ms. Quincy was saying, "is that 'My Future' is the topic for this year's *New York Standard* Student Essay Contest. The best essay from every sixth-grade class in the state will be sent in to the newspaper, and the winning essay will be published for everyone to read!"

Ms. Quincy paused here and glanced around the room with a smile, but her face fell when nobody else looked excited. "You have all heard of the *New York Standard*, I hope?" she asked. "It's only the most-read newspaper in the country."

*But not in East Dumpsford,* Gladys thought.

The teacher brushed chalk dust briskly from her hands. "The deadline for this contest is in February," she continued, "which doesn't leave us much time. In fact, I was surprised to learn that your previous teacher wasn't already working on this project with you. But no matter—we'll write very diligently, and I'm sure that we'll find an excellent class representative."

She beamed at the class again, but everyone just stared back silently.

Finally, in the second row, Leah Klein's hand slowly rose into the air.

"Um, Ms. Quincy?" she said. "Sorry, but no one in East Dumpsford reads the *New York Standard*. Not since . . . well . . . you know."

Ms. Quincy looked down at Leah. "I'm afraid I don't know," she said. "Would you care to explain?"

"Um, well," Leah started, "there was this list, a couple of years ago, in the *Standard*? Of the least desirable places to live in New York State? And, well, East Dumpsford was kind of at the top. Because of the landfill, I guess."

Gladys glanced out the window at the lumpy, trash-filled mountain that loomed over East Dumpsford's rooftops and made the streets smell terrible on hot days. No one in town had ever had much good to say about it—that is, until the *New York Standard* attack. Then it had become "our beloved Mount Dumpsford" and "the grand icon of Dumpsford Township" almost overnight.

"There was a riot!" Jake Wheeler cried gleefully, picking up the story where Leah had left off. "Everyone marched down to the train station and tore out the vending machines that sold the *Standard*!"

"Right," Leah said. "Now no one in town even sells it anymore."

Gladys knew that last bit wasn't exactly the case— Mr. Eng always had a few copies for sale in his shop. But it was true that there weren't many buyers, so he often ended up giving them away. That was how

Gladys first started reading the *Standard*'s Dining section, which came out once a week and was full of intricate recipes and reviews of restaurants in the city. Mr. Eng would always sneak it into her bag somehow if Gladys went to his shop on a Wednesday; once he even wrapped a piece of catfish in it.

"So that's probably why Mrs. Wellchurch didn't want us to enter the contest," Leah was saying. "I don't think anyone entered last year, or the year before, either."

Ms. Quincy had been shaking her head as the tale unfolded. "Well, thank you for telling me," she said. "What an unfortunate situation. Nevertheless, you *will* be entering the contest this year. And did I mention that the winner will also receive a five-hundred-dollar cash prize?"

*This* news finally seemed to provoke the reaction Ms. Quincy was waiting for. A ripple of excitement ran through the classroom. Five hundred dollars! The teacher let the hubbub go on for a few moments before asking everyone to settle down.

"We'll start working on the project this afternoon," she announced, "but if you get any good ideas for an essay throughout the morning, make sure to jot them down in your language arts notebook." Then she picked up the chalk again. "Now, who's ready for some fraction-to-decimal conversion?"

Just like that, the room fell silent.

"I'm joking, I'm joking!" She laughed when she saw the sea of crestfallen faces. "We haven't even taken attendance yet! No math for at least ten minutes."

But Gladys didn't wait—as Ms. Quincy called roll, she did some quick math in her head. Five hundred dollars would more than pay off the fire damages at home. And if she wrote a winning essay about a future that sounded really fun—and had nothing to do with food—maybe her parents would be so proud, they'd release her from her punishment early.

This assignment sounded like just the solution she'd been hoping for.

# Chapter 6

# AN AVALANCHE OF POTATOES

"WHAT WOULD YOU BUY WITH FIVE hundred dollars?" was the question echoing all around the sixth-grade cafeteria table at lunchtime. Nicky McDonald and Peter Yang were talking about the latest video games they would splurge on, and Mira Winters was whispering something to Joanna Rodriguez about a clothes-shopping spree. "*I* would give it all to charity," Gladys heard Charissa Bentley saying. "It's not like my family needs the money."

"What will you write about for the contest, Charissa?" Marti Astin asked.

Charissa laughed. "I'm not telling," she said. "You'd probably steal my idea!"

"Why would I do that?"

Charissa looked at Marti coolly. "Because you're not smart enough to think of your own."

Marti's face turned pink.

"You've probably never had an original idea in your whole life," Charissa continued. "You had to call me this morning just to ask what you should wear to school!"

A few of the kids at that end of the table laughed, and Marti's face turned redder. Gladys, sitting several seats away but just within earshot, was about to feel sorry for her when Marti's expression changed to a smirk. "But Charissa," Marti said, "you know who should have called you this morning? *Ms. Quincy.* Did you *see* her outfit?"

*"I KNOW!"* Charissa squealed. "It's *so* hideous!" Just like that, Marti was back in her good graces, and they leaned in together with Rolanda to pick apart the particular horrors of their new teacher's ensemble.

Across the table from Gladys, Parm Singh rolled her eyes.

To say that Gladys had absolutely no friends at school would be an exaggeration, because she did have Parm. A pessimist and a picky eater, Parm wasn't always the most fun to be around. But she and Gladys had been partners on a lot of class projects in the fourth and fifth grades, which made her the closest thing Gladys had to a school friend. Parm's family went away every year for winter break, though, and Gladys couldn't help but worry that by the time they came back, Parm would have forgotten about her. What's more, this year Parm was in the other sixth-grade class, so they didn't get to see each other much outside of lunch.

Still, it seemed that for now, Parm wanted to talk. She leaned across the table, flicking her long black braid over her shoulder to keep it from dangling into her food, and said quietly, "So it sounds like your new teacher has a fashion problem?"

"Her style is very . . . unique," Gladys told her, reluctant to say anything too bad about a teacher she might actually like. "So," she said, quickly changing the subject, "how was India? Did you try any of the food this time?"

Both of Parm's parents had been born in India, and every winter they packed the entire family onto a plane and went back for two weeks. To Gladys, the trip sounded terribly exotic, but Parm always said it was just plain terrible. The problem was the food. There were only two dishes in the world that Parm liked: cold cereal with milk and plain spaghetti.

Nothing else could tempt her—not even the cookies and snack cakes that other kids traded at lunchtime. Last year, Parm had told their teacher she had strict religious dietary restrictions (even though this wasn't true) just to get out of eating things she didn't like on International Culture Day. Gladys had been both appalled and impressed by Parm's boldness.

Parm's parents had given up trying to change their daughter's eating habits a long time ago. Gladys learned this one night in fifth grade when she stayed at Parm's house for dinner after they worked together on a book report. The Singhs' house was filled with warm, spicy aromas unlike any Gladys had ever smelled, and when the kids were called to the table, Gladys could barely believe the riches displayed there. Parm's older brother Jagmeet said that the crispy-looking, potato-filled triangles were called samosas, then went on to explain what was in the other dishes. A series of huge white bowls contained channa masala (golden-brown chickpeas in a thick, fragrant sauce), palak paneer (bright green pureed spinach with cubes of white cheese), and aloo gobi (potato and cauliflower pieces speckled with mustard seeds and a spice Gladys already knew from Mr. Eng's: cumin). There was also a huge plate of scented white rice, a pile of steaming round breads called rotis, and a bowl of cool yogurt with bits of mint in it called raita.

Gladys's eyes and mouth watered all at once, and she took a seat between Jagmeet and Parm. Jagmeet was already reaching for a samosa, and Gladys was about to do the same when Mrs. Singh came out of the kitchen and plopped two bowls of unadorned spaghetti noodles down in front of the girls.

"Thanks, Mom," said Parm, digging right in. But Gladys didn't touch her noodles.

"Um, if it's all right," Gladys said to Mrs. Singh, "I'd like to have what you're having, please. It smells delicious."

"No it doesn't," Parm said, lifting a forkful of clumped noodles out of her bowl. "It smells gross."

"Parminder *Singh*!" her mother cried. "This young lady is our guest, and she will have whatever she likes!"

Just then, Mr. Singh walked in from the kitchen with a pitcher of water and took his seat at the table, raising his eyebrows at the commotion. Mrs. Singh, meanwhile, grabbed a plate from the sideboard and piled rice onto it with determination.

"You know that I do not like that word," she said to Parm, ladling scoop after scoop of food onto the plate. "What is 'gross,' anyway? It is only your opinion. It is bad enough that you must insult our cooking in front of a guest"—here Mrs. Singh shot Gladys a toothy smile as she reached for a samosa—"but your insult does not carry any weight. Details, Parminder. You know the rule—if you can explain to me why you don't like it, then you don't have to eat it."

Parm groaned, and what came out of her mouth

next sounded dull and practiced, like she'd repeated it hundreds of times. "Samosas too crispy, masala too moist, rice too pointy, raita too slippery. Okay?"

"Okay," Mrs. Singh said with a sigh. "Here, dear." She held the full plate out to Gladys as she sank into a chair.

Gladys stared at the huge pile of food in disbelief. Surely Mrs. Singh couldn't expect her to eat *all* of it, could she?

"Oh, look at this, how ridiculous of me," Mrs. Singh said, pulling the plate back. "I forgot to give you any roti." She reached across the table, grasped two pieces of the browned, flat bread, and layered them on top of Gladys's plate. "There," she said, handing Gladys the plate again. "Enjoy, dear."

Although she couldn't finish even half of it, the dinner Gladys was served at the Singhs' went down as one of the greatest meals of her life. She wrote all about it in her journal the moment she got home.

*When I first saw how much food Mrs. Singh had put on my plate, I couldn't believe my eyes. It smelled amazing, but how was I supposed to eat a mountain of rice with an avalanche of potatoes sliding down it? Not to mention a forest of cauliflower, endless fields of spinach, and a boulder pile of chickpeas? I decided that the best way to climb the peak would be to go in circles: Start by using the roti like a shovel to pick up some chickpeas, then dig into the rice mountain with a fork(lift) . . .*

Gladys went on to describe how the samosa shell did a good job of soaking up the extra chickpea gravy, and how the minty yogurt cooled her mouth down when the spices tickling her tongue threatened to turn into a tornado. Before she knew it, she had written three whole pages, wrapping the review up with an exuberant:

★★★✦ *(setting the standard for all dinners to come!)*

After particularly horrible meals the following year, Gladys would turn back to her review and reread it to relive that glorious feast. In this way, she could sometimes trick herself into thinking her indigestion was from too many spicy chickpeas and crunchy samosas, instead of from the rubbery chicken nuggets she'd eaten for dinner or the mystery-meat sandwiches her parents packed her for lunch.

Gladys forced herself to bite into one such sandwich now. The slimy meat had no flavor other than salt, and her mom's favorite fat-free mayonnaise oozed through the squishy white bread.

"India was all right," Parm told her. "The first week was pretty boring, but then my cousin got married, and the parties went on for days! There must have been a thousand guests there. Everyone would dance, and then eat, and then dance some more. And you should have seen the food. There was more of it than I've ever seen in my life."

"Did you eat any?" Gladys asked excitedly.

Parm gave her a funny look. "Of course not," she said. "But it *looked* very pretty."

Gladys sighed. It amazed her that there were people in the world who ate the kind of food Parm's parents cooked every day, and it amazed her even more that Parm had a chance to be one of them and declined. But after a disastrous trip to India when Parm was six and lost almost ten pounds, her parents had stopped trying to change her. Now they packed an enormous extra suitcase full of Apple Snax, Wheaty Squares, Choco-Rings, powdered milk, and boxed spaghetti for the family's trips across the world, despite the shame it brought upon them in the eyes of their relatives.

Parm took another bite of the cereal she'd brought for lunch and looked like she might be about to ask Gladys how *her* vacation had been. So Gladys quickly asked her, "What do you think of this essay contest?" Apparently, Ms. Quincy had convinced Parm's teacher to participate this year, too.

"I think it's a big waste of time," Parm said, crunching on her last Choco-Ring. "Do you know how many elementary schools there are in this state? *Thousands.*

Even if you wrote the best essay in your class, your chances of winning would be tiny."

"But," said Gladys, "somebody has to win, don't they?"

Parm shrugged. "I guess."

As they lined up for recess after the bell rang, Gladys's mind was still on the contest—or, more specifically, the prize money. After she paid for new curtains, she might even have enough left over to buy herself one of those fancy stand mixers like the chefs on Planet Food used.

They reached the playground, and Gladys's classmates broke off into their cliques and headed for different areas. Even Parm, who played in a soccer league after school, had a small group to run drills or play two-on-two with during recess. She was at least polite enough to wave good-bye as she ran to the far field. Everyone else ignored Gladys, leaving her alone at her usual spot by the fence.

*That's okay,* she told herself, pulling her journal and pencil out of her coat pocket. *I really need the time to think of a good essay topic.*

But it was hard to think of the future without thinking about food. Ever since she'd read her first Dining section, Gladys had known what she wanted to be when she grew up—the restaurant critic for the *New York Standard.* She would eat incredible meals all over New York City and write about them for millions of people to read. She would probably have to eat some bad meals, too, but at least then her reviews could help other people avoid eating the same awful things she had.

She couldn't write about that for the contest, though. It definitely wouldn't get her back into her parents' good graces, and it would probably cause her classmates to upgrade her status from Weird Quiet Kid to Total Freak. She'd seen the way they'd made fun of Parm last year when she turned down a Sticky Meal at the end-of-year party. (Gladys had taken one for appearance's sake, then slipped it into the trash when no one was looking.) What if the other kids found out that Gladys not only hated fast food, but also wanted to work for East Dumpsford's least favorite newspaper when she grew up? That would be like icing on the Cake of Social Doom.

## Chapter 7

# SEVENTEEN WAYS TO COOK A CARROT

GLADYS'S MOM DROPPED HER OFF AT home that afternoon, warned her not to cook, and headed back to the office for a few more hours of work. Miraculously, Gladys's parents had given her one more chance to prove that she could take care of herself. But they would be checking the kitchen carefully for signs that she was back to her old cooking habits . . . and if they found any, new punishments would be handed out, and an after-school babysitter would be called in.

Gladys settled in at her usual spot at the kitchen table and tried to attack her homework, but it was hard to concentrate. Everything around her felt like a reminder of the crème brûlée disaster:

★ ★ ★ ★

the singed countertop, the taped-over stove burners. Even the sunlight streaming in through the window seemed to say "Hey, remember when there were curtains here?"

And then there was the refrigerator door, where her parents had stuck up two lists:

<u>APPROVED ACTIVITIES</u>
    Video games
    Computer games
    Watching TV (but no cooking shows!)
    Reading (but not cookbooks!)
    Bike riding
    Hanging out at the mall
    Snowball fighting
    Microwaving (with supervision)

<u>UNAPPROVED ACTIVITIES</u>
    Cooking
    Using power tools
    Anything else adults do that kids normally don't

The kitchen was Gladys's favorite room in the house, but this was all just too depressing. She headed upstairs to the window seat with her language arts notebook and stared outside, hoping for some inspiration for her essay. That's when she noticed Sandy Anderson playing alone in his backyard. There was still a small pile of snow from a storm the week before, and he was scooping handfuls off the top, packing them into balls, and hurling them against the back of his house.

He seemed to be having fun. And snowball fighting was actually on her list of approved activities. *Maybe if I try new things,* Gladys thought, *I'll get new ideas.* Before she knew it, her boots and coat were back on and she was outside in her own backyard.

Cautiously, she approached the low hedge that divided the Gatsbys' property from the Andersons'. It was easy to see over, even for someone of Gladys's height (or Sandy's, who was a couple of inches shorter than Gladys). She kept hoping that Sandy would look up from his one-man snowball fight and notice her, and she tried to think of what to say when he did. But he was so focused that he didn't even look up when Gladys was standing right next to the hedge.

"Hey!" Gladys finally called as Sandy wound up for another throw. "Think you can hit me?"

Sandy turned toward her, and a look of dread crossed his face. Instead of throwing the snowball in his hand, he turned and fled toward his back door without a word, the snow slipping out of his mitten and plopping onto the grass.

Unfortunately, Sandy's mother was coming out the door just as Sandy was about to go in, and they collided with a smack. As they backed away from each other, Mrs. Anderson rubbing her elbow and Sandy muttering "Sorry, Mom," Mrs. Anderson caught sight of Gladys standing near the hedge.

"Well, hello there, neighbor!" she called, waving. "Look, Sandy, it's the girl from next door. Have you said hello to her?"

Mrs. Anderson beamed a warm smile in Gladys's direction. She was a slightly plump lady with dark blond hair that fell in curls down her back, and today she was wearing a tie-dyed apron over a sweatshirt and a pair of stretchy yoga pants. She held a spatula in her hand.

"Hello," Sandy mumbled in Gladys's general direction without making eye contact. He still looked scared.

"Hi," Gladys said awkwardly. Sandy's behavior was very confusing, but she tried not to take it personally. Maybe he was just shy. Still, she found herself wishing that she had never come outside in the first place.

As Gladys stood there, wondering how long she would have to wait before she could make her escape, Mrs. Anderson got the worst idea in the world.

"I have the best idea in the world!" she said. "Sandy, why don't you invite our neighbor over to play?"

Of course, Gladys had come outside hoping that Sandy might want to play, but having his mother tell him to ask was just too humiliating. Gladys was relieved when Sandy told his mom that he was ready to go inside.

"Then ask her to come in, too!" Mrs. Anderson replied. "That way I won't have to listen to you complain about how bored you are without anyone to hang out with!"

"Um," said Sandy. "Um . . ." It was clear that he saw no way out of the situation. Finally he looked at Gladys and said very quickly, "Doyouwannacomeover?"

Now Gladys had a choice to make: Go home for another solitary hour, or go next door with a kid who didn't really want her there. Neither option seemed too appealing.

"Do you need to check with your parents first?" Mrs. Anderson asked.

"That's okay," Gladys replied. "They're both at work 'til six."

"Well, you're very welcome at our house."

*Oh, what the heck,* Gladys thought. At the very least, it would be a change of scenery. She stepped through a gap in the hedge and crossed over toward the Andersons' back door.

The inside of their house was warm and smelled like chocolate. Gladys's mouth watered.

"I just took some brownies out of the oven," Mrs. Anderson said as she led Gladys and Sandy down a hallway. "So when you kids are hungry, you should come to the kitchen and have a snack!" She ushered them through a doorway and into a large room filled with toys and games. There was a brightly colored skateboard propped up against one wall, a squashy beanbag chair in the corner, a mini Ping-Pong table, *and* a mini pool table.

Still, neither Gladys nor Sandy was too happy when Mrs. Anderson instructed them to "have fun" and disappeared down the hallway. Gladys would have preferred to go with Mrs. Anderson, to have a look around her kitchen and sample one of her brownies, and Sandy's face returned to looking terrified. They were standing near the doorway, eyeing each other, when a scuffling sound from the corner of the playroom made Gladys jump. She looked over to where the noise was coming from and saw a large wooden hutch with not one, but two eager-looking balls of fluff pressing their paws against the wire-mesh door.

"You have rabbits!" she cried. Gladys loved animals and had always wanted a pet. But because of her father's allergies, anything with fur was out of the question—and it seemed to Gladys that all of the pets worth having had fur.

Unfortunately, the sight of Gladys's excitement made Sandy more petrified, if this was even possible. In fact, he was starting to look downright panicky. Gladys wondered what she could do to calm him down. Maybe playing with the pets would do the trick. "What are their names?" she asked gently, approaching the rabbits' hutch.

Sandy trailed after her. He cleared his throat a

couple of times and finally managed to find his voice. "Um, this one's Edward Hopper," he squeaked, "and that one is his brother, Dennis."

Gladys peered through the wire to get a good look at the rabbits. Edward was mostly white, but had perky black ears and thick black rims around his eyes, as if he'd gotten into Mrs. Anderson's mascara. Dennis, on the other hand, was brown and had floppy ears. Dennis was also twice as big as Edward.

"Are you sure they're brothers?" Gladys asked.

"Th-that's what my mom says," Sandy said shakily.

"Well," Gladys said with a laugh, "don't believe everything your *parents* tell you."

Gladys could see immediately that this had been the wrong thing to say—Sandy looked very alarmed at the idea that a parent could possibly be wrong about anything.

After another incredibly long silence, Gladys finally asked, "Can I pet them?"

Sandy looked positively ill at this notion. "Um, they're not supposed to come out of the cage," he mumbled, looking away.

Just then, Mrs. Anderson reappeared in the doorway. "How are you kids doing?" she asked. "Sandy, why don't you show Gladys that trick you've been working on with Edward Hopper? What, you haven't even taken them out yet?" She strode toward the hutch and, in one motion, released the latch and swung open the wire door. "They're usually out of the cage the moment he walks in the room!" she told Gladys. "Don't be shy!" she whispered to Sandy. Then, closing the door so the rabbits couldn't get out into the hallway, Mrs. Anderson left them alone together again.

Gladys looked at Sandy. She was trying to think of a way to ask why he had lied to her about the rabbits when he blurted, "I saw you at Mr. Eng's grocery store!"

"What?" said Gladys.

"Don't play dumb! I heard what you were asking him for!"

"I've asked Mr. Eng for a lot of things," Gladys said truthfully. "You'll have to be more specific."

Sandy looked away. Edward Hopper had already shot out of the cage and was hopping around the room, but Dennis Hopper had only made it as far as Sandy's feet. Sandy bent down and scooped him up. Dennis Hopper wriggled and kicked his legs, but Sandy was not letting go.

"Meat," Sandy finally managed to whisper. "R-rabbit meat."

Suddenly, it all made sense. A few months back, Gladys had found a recipe for a French dish called lapin à la cocotte in her cookbook *Tender Is the Meat* and asked Mr. Eng if he had any rabbit. He didn't, but he told her he could order some if she really wanted it.

When she found out how much it would cost, though, she told him not to bother and soon forgot about that recipe altogether.

Dennis Hopper continued to struggle, but Sandy held on tight. "I've seen you through the window, cooking in your kitchen," he said, his voice more confident now, "making all sorts of weird . . . stews and things. Well, you're not getting your hands on the Hoppers!"

As if on cue, Dennis gave a mighty kick and managed to free himself from Sandy's grip, leaping to the floor. "Dennis!" Sandy cried, lurching after him, but Dennis had scampered off to join Edward in wedging himself between the beanbag chair and the wall at the far corner of the room.

Gladys couldn't help herself—she laughed.

"What's so funny?" Sandy asked sharply.

"You really thought that I would steal your rabbits? And cook them?" she said between giggles. "These aren't even the kinds of rabbits people eat! I mean, look at Edward; he's hardly got an ounce of meat on him!"

Sandy looked over at Edward, who was now trying to dig a hole in the beanbag chair with his tiny paws. "I don't know," he said. "I read that some people in South America eat guinea pigs, and Edward is bigger than a guinea pig."

This was true, and Gladys began to wonder if Sandy

might actually be smarter than she had given him credit for. She stopped laughing.

"Well," she said huffily, "I would never cook some-one's *pets*. Besides," she added with a sigh, "I'm not allowed to cook anymore—I've been banned from the kitchen."

Sandy's eyebrows lifted slightly. "Really? How come?"

The story came gushing out of Gladys like milk spilling from a busted carton. "It was so unfair," she concluded. "It could have happened to anyone! But now my parents say that if I'm caught even boiling water, I'll be grounded for life."

Gladys stared down at her salmon-hued sneakers, which looked like they were swimming on the surface of the shaggy blue carpet. She wasn't sure why she'd just told this boy about the accident; maybe it felt okay because he didn't go to her school.

"You set your curtains on *fire*?"

Gladys nodded miserably—but Sandy seemed to have the opposite reaction.

"Wow," he said. "That's so cool! Man, anyone at my school who did that would be a total celebrity!"

"They would?" Now Gladys wondered if Sandy went to a reform school.

Sandy grinned. "Maybe it's 'cause my school is all boys. I guess girls can be more, uh, sensory about that kind of stuff."

"Do you mean *sensitive*?" Gladys asked.

"Yeah, sensitive. Listen, do you want to try this computer program I just invented? It's called Rabbit Race."

"Sure!" Gladys followed him across the room and waited as the computer screen buzzed to life. Two boxy-looking rabbit icons appeared at the bottom— one fat and brown like Dennis, the other small and spotted like Edward.

"You have to get your guy through the maze to the carrot," Sandy explained, pointing to the mess of lines on the screen and the orange stick at its center. "One of us can use the arrow keys and the other can use the mouse."

"You made this game yourself?" Gladys asked.

"Well, my mom helped," Sandy said. "She's a computer programmer and works from home."

"Still, that's really impressive," Gladys said, and she meant it.

Sandy shrugged. "It's just what I like to do. But lately my mom's started yelling at me to get off the computer and play outside and stuff. She says there'll be plenty of time for programming when I'm older."

Gladys nodded. "That sounds a *lot* like my parents."

"So, do you wanna be Dennis or Edward?" Sandy asked. "I'll let you pick since it's your first time playing."

Gladys chose Edward, who was controlled by the mouse, and soon her rabbit was racing through the maze onscreen. Dennis beat her to the carrot by just a few seconds, and his pixelated cottontail wagged triumphantly.

"Good job!" Gladys said.

Sandy's ears turned a little red as he smiled. "Well, it's not really a fair match. I did design the whole maze. Wanna play again?"

"Sure," Gladys said, "but then after, maybe we can play with the real rabbits?"

"How about this: Rabbit Race, then we eat brownies, then real rabbits."

"Deal!"

Gladys won the second round of Rabbit Race, though she thought Sandy may have taken a wrong turn on purpose. Then they trooped down the hall to the kitchen, where Mrs. Anderson was slicing brownies into thick squares.

The kitchen was a mess. Flour dusted the countertops, and the sink was bursting with batter-coated bowls and utensils. Cookbooks were stuffed haphazardly into a bookcase along the wall, many of their spines cracked from use.

It was the most beautiful room Gladys had ever seen.

"I've been experimenting with different flavors," Mrs. Anderson said as she handed Gladys and Sandy each a brownie. "These are butterscotch-nutmeg. What do you think?"

"Thanksh, Mom," Sandy said, his mouth already full. "Itsh aweshome."

Gladys took a bite of her brownie, and a slew of flavors flooded her taste buds. The sweet, melty butterscotch offset the bitterness of the chocolate, and the hint of nutmeg gave the whole thing a kick. It was very tasty—but still, as Gladys swallowed, she felt like something was missing.

"Do you know that extra-fancy Vietnamese cinnamon Mr. Eng sells?" she blurted. "I think a touch of that in the batter would really help balance things out."

Mrs. Anderson's eyes widened in surprise, and even Sandy stopped chewing and gave Gladys a funny look.

"I mean, it's terrific—thank you so much," she mumbled.

But Mrs. Anderson was shaking her head now. "You know, I think you may be right!" She turned back to the counter and rummaged through the spice rack until she found the jar she wanted. "Now let's see . . ." She sprinkled a bit of the cinnamon onto her half-eaten brownie and took another bite. "Yes, that's perfect!" she cried. She turned back to Gladys. "How did you know?"

Gladys glanced over at Sandy. He pretended to wipe his chocolate-smeared mouth, but really drew his fingers across his lips in a zipping motion, as if to say, *Your cooking secrets are safe with me.*

"Oh, I just heard Mr. Eng talking about it at the store," she said. "He said it would be good in any dessert." Technically, that was true—she'd just left out the part where she'd experimented with the cinnamon herself in more than forty recipes.

"Well, I'm glad you remembered," Mrs. Anderson said. "I'll have to make a note of that on my recipe for next time." She pulled a slim book out of the cookbookcase, which caused all of the other ones on that shelf to shift. The last book in the row—an enormous, dark blue volume—tumbled to the floor with a thud.

*"The Larousse Gastronomique!"* Gladys could barely suppress a squeal. It was *the* original French cookbook, with over a thousand pages of classic recipes. Gladys had paged through it at the library, but could never convince her parents to buy the expensive book, not even for her birthday and Christmas combined.

"Yes," Mrs. Anderson said, kneeling to pick up the hefty tome. "It was my grandmother's, the original English translation. I probably don't take care of it like I should."

Gladys shook her head. "Cookbooks are meant to be used. I don't think they should be kept on a shelf looking pretty."

Mrs. Anderson bit her lip thoughtfully. "That's very wise. Sandy, I think your new friend has a lot more cooking experience than she's letting on!"

Gladys looked over at Sandy, who shrugged non-committally and swallowed his last bite of brownie. "Mom, can we take a carrot in for the Hoppers?"

"Sure, honey." Mrs. Anderson turned back to Gladys. "Would you like to take a closer look at the *Larousse*?"

A warm, happy feeling coursed through Gladys, like the kind you get from a sip of hot cider on the first cold day of fall. "I'd love to," she said.

And so, a minute later, Gladys was following Sandy back down the hall, staggering under the weight of the huge cookbook. They spent the rest of the afternoon playing with the Hoppers and flipping through the cookbook's pages. Sandy showed Gladys his trick of getting Edward Hopper to "walk" on his hind legs by dangling a carrot over the rabbit's nose, and Gladys, with the help of the *Larousse,* showed Sandy seventeen different ways to cook that carrot, if he was ever so inclined.

# Chapter 8

# AN UNFORTUNATE MESS

"GLADYS," MS. QUINCY SAID QUIETLY. It was silent reading time, and the teacher was patrolling the aisles as usual. Gladys had been absorbed in her book about a radiant, humble pig and hadn't noticed Ms. Quincy sneaking up behind her. "I'd like to speak with you after class."

Gladys swallowed. Her mouth felt like she'd just eaten a boxful of crackers and was all out of milk. Unable to speak, she nodded.

"Very good," Ms. Quincy whispered, and she moved on down the aisle without another word.

Ms. Quincy had been their teacher for three weeks now, and so far Gladys

★ ★ ★ ★

thought she was a huge improvement over Mrs. Well-church. She'd even set up a suggestion box on her desk, where students could submit their own ideas for activities or lessons. Gladys hadn't seen anyone use it yet, but she liked that her teacher was open to their opinions.

But why did Ms. Quincy want to see her after class? She didn't think she could be in trouble, but still, she could hardly concentrate on her book for the last ten minutes of the school day.

When the bell finally rang, the kids around her leapt out of their seats and noisily started gathering their things. Gladys packed her lobster backpack carefully, dragging the process out pencil by pencil until the classroom was empty.

"Gladys, grab a chair and have a seat," Ms. Quincy said, pointing to the spot next to her own chair behind the desk. "I have your essay, 'My Future as a Veterinarian,' here."

Gladys had gotten the idea while she was playing with the Hoppers at Sandy's house, and had handed her essay in that Monday with the rest of the class. But Ms. Quincy said that they wouldn't get them back until the following week, and it was only Wednesday now. Gladys's breath caught in her throat as her teacher turned over the piece of paper on her desk. It was covered with red ink.

Ms. Quincy seemed to read her mind. "Now, don't be put off by all the red marks," she said. "Your writing has a lot of potential. With a little help, I think that you could have an excellent chance of winning the *New York Standard* contest."

"Oh," Gladys said, taken aback. She was having trouble reconciling what she saw on the marked-up page with the words that were coming out of her teacher's mouth.

Ms. Quincy removed her glasses and picked up the paper. "This is actually a very good essay, Gladys. It has strong descriptions and some truly lovely metaphors. There's really only one problem." She laid the paper back down on the desk and turned to look Gladys in the eye. "I don't believe a word of it."

Gladys's heart plummeted like a too-dense matzo ball in a pot of soup.

"What's missing here," Ms. Quincy continued matter-of-factly, "is passion. Tell me, Gladys—do you *really* want to be a veterinarian when you grow up?"

"I love animals," Gladys said in a small voice.

Ms. Quincy leaned in closer. "And there's nothing else you love more?"

Gladys didn't respond, and the teacher sat up straighter. "I'll be returning the rest of the class's essays next week," she said, "but I'd like to give you a chance to rewrite yours if you want. Whatever you decide, you can hand in your final essay on Friday." She passed Gladys the marked-up paper.

"And I have something else for you," the teacher added. She reached into her briefcase and pulled out a sealed envelope. "It's something that I wrote. Have you ever heard of a cover letter before?"

Gladys shook her head no.

"I thought you might not have," Ms. Quincy said. "It's a special kind of letter that adults write when they're applying for a new job. I think it might help you understand what I mean about passion." She handed Gladys the envelope. "Now, I don't think I need to remind you that this is a private letter that is not meant to be passed around to other students." Ms. Quincy raised one eyebrow, and Gladys shook her head vigorously.

"Very well, you may go now," Ms. Quincy said, placing her glasses back across her nose. Then she smiled and her eyes lit up behind the lenses. "And good luck!"

On the way home, Gladys pedaled her bike furiously. Her mind was racing, too. Ms. Quincy seemed to see right through her, and Gladys didn't know whether to be mad about that or glad. Of course she wanted to write the best essay she could to win that five hundred dollars . . . but at the same time, the thought of her parents—and everyone at school— reading that her true passion was *food* made her feel so nauseous that she wasn't sure she'd ever be able to eat again.

*And what's the deal with this secret letter?* Gladys thought as she skidded around the corner. Would reading it really be able to help her figure things out?

She had the envelope in her hand the moment she'd parked her bike in the garage, but for some reason she was too nervous to open it. Not knowing what else to do, she crossed the lawn and rang Sandy's doorbell.

Over the last few weeks, Gladys had been going over to Sandy's almost every day after school. Not only was it much more fun than hanging out alone, but it made her parents happy, too. Ever since they'd found out that she had a new friend—and that it was a *boy,* who was surely not interested in cooking—they'd barely been able to contain their enthusiasm.

"Whatsh up?" Sandy asked, stepping out onto the front porch with a full mouth. "Wanna cookie?"

Gladys was tempted, but her stomach was doing too many flip-flops for food. "I have this letter from my teacher—" she started.

"Ooh, are you in trouble?" Sandy asked.

"No!" Gladys said. "It's supposed to help me with this essay I have to write, somehow. But she said it's private . . . I'm not supposed to show it to anyone else."

"Aw, man."

"Well, anyone else in my *class,* actually . . ." Gladys continued. "I mean, I think it would be okay if I showed it to you. You don't even go to my school."

"Let's see!" Sandy said, grabbing the envelope out of Gladys's hand. In one swift movement, he tore it open.

"Hey!" Gladys cried (but secretly, she was glad he'd opened it).

Sandy handed Gladys a single sheet of cream-colored stationery. As she unfolded it, Sandy leaned in to read over her shoulder. The letter said:

*Violetta Quincy*
*violetta.quincy@worldmail.com*

*Rafael Brinkley*
*Principal*
*East Dumpsford Elementary School*
*328 Landfill View Road*
*East Dumpsford, NY 11573*

*Dear Mr. Brinkley:*

*I am writing you to apply for the position of sixth-grade teacher, which I saw advertised online. I am sure you will agree that I am well-qualified for the job.*

"Pretty boring so far," said Sandy.
"Shhh!" said Gladys.

*As the daughter of aid workers, I grew up in the small African nation of Togo and was educated by my parents in a one-room schoolhouse through the age of twelve.*

"Wow!" said Sandy.
"I knew it would get better," Gladys said.

*I was then sent to an elite boarding school in Switzerland as a teenager. At sixteen, I chose to attend the University of Hong Kong to work on my Cantonese, and finally I completed a graduate program in teaching at City College in New York.*

*I have had a passion for education since the earliest days of my own childhood. As a young girl, I did chores for my Togolese friends so that they could have more time to study in the schoolhouse. In my teenage years, I volunteered to tutor local Swiss children who could not afford to attend my academy. I believe strongly in every child's right to learn as much as he or she possibly can and have always been willing to do everything within my power to help them.*

*As you know, Mr. Brinkley, East Dumpsford's*
*schools have a reputation for being among*
*the weakest in the county. To remedy this*
*situation, I plan to continue doing what I have*
*always done, which is to grant my students*
*the personal attention they deserve. In this*
*manner I am quite sure that I can help bring*
*East Dumpsford Elementary up to scratch,*
*eventually turning it into one of the finest*
*schools in the area.*

*I look forward to hearing back from you about*
*this opportunity.*

*Sincerely,*
*Violetta Quincy*

"That explains why she didn't want you to show it
to anyone else, at least," Sandy said. "She must not
want the other kids to know what she really thinks
about your school."

"I guess so," Gladys agreed.

"Well," Sandy said, "your school might suck, but it
sounds like you've got a pretty cool teacher! She lived
in Africa and China and stuff!"

Gladys had to agree—and now she was thinking
about all of the yummy international recipes Ms.
Quincy might know from her travels.

"So how is this supposed to help with your essay?" Sandy asked, taking another bite of cookie.

Gladys sighed. "It's supposed to inspire me, I think. She said that my essay doesn't have any passion—she doesn't believe I really want to be a vet."

Sandy let out a hoot of laughter, spraying cookie crumbs all over the porch. "A vet? I thought you wanted to be a food writer. You'd be so good at it—that journal entry you read me about the pork chops was hilarious!"

Gladys jammed her hands deep into her coat pockets. It was a nice thing to say, but she wished that Sandy hadn't mentioned her journal. She'd never considered showing an entry to anyone before she met him . . . but when her parents actually followed through on their promise to start cooking more, she'd needed to share the horrifying results with *someone*. She'd written this entry a few days earlier:

*The pork chop, though burnt around the edges, still oozed blood from its center. The peas, which had been microwaved past the point of bursting, arrived at the table in a soggy, mushy state fit for a baby. And someone obviously forgot to add the instant potato flakes to the mashed potatoes, which led to an unfortunate mess of melted margarine, hot milk, and salt being ladled onto my plate by*

*the absentminded server, who was talking on her*
*cell phone at the time.*

Not wanting to be too mean, though, she'd added,

> *The ice cream that ~~Dad~~ the chef ~~brought home~~*
> ~~*from the store*~~ *selected for dessert was pretty*
> *good.*
>
> ⟿ *(saved by the ice cream)*

The day after that meal, Gladys had brought her journal over to Sandy's house. Once he heard that review, he insisted on reading more. She'd been happy that he liked her writing, but now she wasn't so sure that sharing had been a good idea. Having him remind her of her *real* career goal—the one she couldn't write about in her essay—was the last thing she needed right now. What she needed was to prove to Ms. Quincy, and her parents, and the *New York Standard* that she really, really wanted to become a vet.

Sandy didn't seem to get that, though. "Have you written any new reviews?" he asked excitedly. "What did your mom pack you for lunch today?"

"Can't we talk about anything other than food?" Gladys snapped. The words came out harsher than she'd meant them to, but she just needed Sandy to stop going on about her reviews. Her outburst seemed to have worked—Sandy's mouth was hanging open now, but no more sounds were coming out.

His blue eyes were watering, though, like he'd just sniffed a jarful of hot peppers.

*Fudge,* Gladys thought. Food was getting her into nothing but trouble these days. Maybe she really *should* become a vet!

Feeling her cheeks grow warm, Gladys shuffled backward toward the edge of the porch. She knew that she should apologize, but when she opened her mouth again, all that came out was, "I've got to start my homework." Then, turning away, she jumped down the steps and took off across the lawn.

# Chapter 9

# MEATBRAIN

A COLD GUST OF WIND WHIPPED ACROSS the yard as Gladys jogged back to her house. *Sandy just doesn't understand how much is riding on this contest,* she thought. His mom might shoo him away from the computer sometimes, but she had never all-out banned him from his favorite activity. Gladys's parents would never let her back in the kitchen unless they believed that she had other interests in life, too.

At home, Gladys wandered around the kitchen, poking through the cupboards in search of a snack. But all she found was the old box of energy bars from her first day back at school. There was a faded picture of a mountain biker on the

★ ★ ★ ★

box, which seemed fitting to Gladys, since the bars tasted like gravel.

Wishing now that she *had* taken a cookie from next door, Gladys climbed the stairs to her parents' home office. She turned on the computer and settled into the enormous swivel chair. Maybe she could change the format of her essay and write it like a cover letter applying for a veterinary job. That probably wasn't what Ms. Quincy was expecting, but it might impress her a little anyway.

The monitor came to life, and the log-in page for DumpMail popped up automatically. DumpMail was the local e-mail service that everyone in town used, including Gladys's parents. Gladys knew that most of the kids at school had DumpMail accounts because she sometimes heard them talking about the Instant DumpMessages they sent to one another.

Gladys didn't have an account, but this had never seemed like a big deal to her, since she didn't have friends to e-mail with anyway. She would have liked to e-mail with Aunt Lydia, but her aunt didn't believe in the Internet. She said it disturbed the vibrations of the universe, or something, so they stuck to letters and phone calls.

But looking at the heading on Ms. Quincy's letter, Gladys saw that real professionals had e-mail addresses. And if she wanted her letter/essay to show that she was serious about becoming a vet, she'd better have one, too.

With a click on the *Sign up now!* link and a few quick keystrokes, the task was done. Gladys made sure to choose a professional-looking e-mail address (ggatsby@dumpmail.com), rather than a silly one like her dad's (kookycpa@dumpmail.com) or her mom's (iluvtosellhouses4u@dumpmail.com).

Next, Gladys had to will herself not to open a new window and surf directly to the *New York Standard* website. It was Wednesday, the day that new reviews and recipes came out in the Dining section, and she liked to look at them online when she couldn't get a paper copy at Mr. Eng's. But instead she opened a new document and typed her name and new e-mail address in the upper right-hand corner. Then, looking between the screen, Ms. Quincy's neatly typed letter, and her own marked-up paper, she began to rewrite "My Future as a Veterinarian."

She was a couple of paragraphs in when the will to keep going failed her. Ms. Quincy was right—the essay was boring. Passionless. But how could she fix it? She stared at the screen, but no great ideas came to her. She was considering picking a new fake future profession—pro cyclist?—when the doorbell rang.

Grateful for an excuse to take a break, Gladys leapt out of the swivel chair and bounded down the stairs.

But her excitement faded when she looked out the peephole and saw Sandy and his mom standing on the porch.

She knew that she'd been rude to Sandy earlier. Had they come over to force her to apologize? Sheepishly, Gladys opened the door.

"Hello, Gladys!" Mrs. Anderson said. She didn't seem like she was angry. Her hands were tying an orange bandanna over her curly hair. "I just got called in as an emergency sub at the yoga studio, so I gave your mom a ring at her office. She said it would be fine to drop Sandy off here."

Sandy didn't look particularly thrilled. "I tried to tell her that I'm old enough to stay home alone," he said.

"Not 'til you're eleven," Mrs. Anderson insisted, adjusting the yoga mat that was strapped across her back. "Besides, I didn't have time to make you dinner, and Gladys's mom was nice enough to invite you to eat with them. Isn't that great? She said they were going to make a meatloaf."

Gladys felt the blood drain from her face. "Great" was *not* the word she'd use to describe this situation. She'd been avoiding inviting Sandy to her house precisely to save him from her parents' cooking.

Sandy, on the other hand, suddenly seemed excited. "Dinner here? Excellent!"

Mrs. Anderson leaned down to give him a peck on

the cheek. "Be good," she said, then she dashed across the lawn to her car.

Sandy turned to face Gladys. "So, can I come in?"

Gladys moved aside to let Sandy step into the foyer. "I thought your mom was a computer programmer," she said.

"She teaches yoga, too," Sandy told her as he shrugged out of his coat. "Just usually while I'm at band or karate."

"Look," Gladys said, "you don't have to eat the meatloaf. You can just tell my parents you're a vegetarian. Or that you're allergic to ground meat, or something."

Sandy laughed. *"No way!* I want to try one of these famous Gatsby dinners for myself!"

He set off toward the living room, and Gladys scurried after him. "I don't think you understand what awful cooks my parents are," she said.

"Yeah, well, sometimes my mom tries to teach me how to cook stuff, and I'm not so good, either. But I haven't died yet from eating stuff I've made." He flopped down onto the sofa and grabbed Gladys's tablet computer from the coffee table.

"I bet that compared to my parents, you're Jacques Pépin," Gladys said.

Sandy was busy swiping at the screen. "The submarine guy?"

"What? No, that's Jacques Cousteau! Jacques

Pépin is a chef, a really great— Ugh, it doesn't matter." Gladys collapsed onto the sofa next to him. "My dad, when he's shopping? He only buys whatever's on sale. So this meat, it'll be all brown and oozy because it's almost expired. And it's probably full of bacteria—which won't get killed, because they don't even know how long to cook it. I'm telling you, it's gonna be super gross!"

Sandy glanced up from the tablet and gave Gladys a huge grin. "I know," he said. "But I'm a boy. I like gross stuff!"

"I give up," Gladys muttered as Sandy turned back to the game he was playing. "But when you're in the hospital with E. coli, don't say I didn't warn you."

A car door slammed outside, and Gladys slumped back farther into the sofa. Sandy may have been in denial, but she wasn't. The countdown to their last moments of friendship had officially begun.

Her parents appeared in the doorway a minute later, a bagful of groceries rustling on her dad's arm.

"Hey, there!" her mom cried. "Are you kids having fun?"

"I'm glad to see that someone's using that thing," her dad said, nodding toward Sandy. "Well, other than me, of course. Gladdy never seems to want to play with it."

"Yeah, it's pretty sweet," Sandy said, glancing up

from the screen. "But my mom won't let me have one. She says I spend too much time on the computer already."

Gladys's dad chuckled. "Our Gladdy seems to have the opposite problem. But maybe you can get her more interested, show her what that thing can do!"

Gladys groaned under her breath. She knew perfectly well what it could do—she'd used it plenty of times in the kitchen, propping it up against the toaster while she looked up recipes or watched instructional cooking videos. But she'd never let her parents know that.

"Well, we'd better go and start dinner," her mom said. "I wonder how long a meatloaf takes to cook?"

"Oh, I don't think there's any set amount of time," said her dad, loosening his tie with his free hand. "We'll just nuke it until it looks done!"

Gladys elbowed Sandy in the arm. "Do you see what I mean?" she hissed. But he just smiled. Only Gladys seemed to understand that he was hurtling toward disaster, just like the poor virtual birds he kept flinging across the tablet screen.

Thirty minutes later, Gladys and Sandy were sitting at the dining room table. The Gatsbys usually ate dinner in front of the TV, but with a guest to impress, Gladys's parents were making a little extra effort. While she and Sandy were playing that bird game (it *was* sort of fun, she had to admit), Gladys's dad had been rummaging around in the crawl space under the stairs. Now the table was laid with china that Gladys had never seen before, and her parents were marching in from the kitchen with a steaming casserole dish held between them.

"Dinner is served!" they announced together.

Sandy leaned forward to look at the dish. "Excellent!" Then, just loud enough for Gladys to hear, he whispered, "It looks like a *brain*!"

Gladys didn't want to look, but once she did, she couldn't tear her eyes away. In the casserole dish was a misshapen, gray lump of meat covered with a mound of pale, quivering gloop that she could only guess was supposed to be gravy.

"See, there's the gray matter," Sandy whispered, "and there's the white—"

*"Shut up!"* Gladys hissed, pushing herself back in her chair. "I think I might be sick."

The microwave's distinctive *ding!* sounded from the kitchen. "That'll be the potato puffs," Gladys's dad said, hurrying off to retrieve them. Gladys breathed a small sigh of relief. Even if you microwaved them, you couldn't really mess up frozen potato puffs, right?

Wrong. When her dad came back carrying a bowl full of mush, it was clear that great harm had befallen the poor puffs. A closer look revealed that the smashed-up potato nuggets were covered with the same whitish gloop that was dripping off the meat.

"This one's a George Gatsby original," he announced proudly. "Mashed potato puffs with gravy!"

"Ooh, George, how creative!" Gladys's mom cried.

Gladys, meanwhile, thought about the buttery, silky-smooth mashed potatoes she'd made just a few weeks ago—using golden spuds, fresh cream, and a delicate sprinkling of sage—and wanted to cry.

"Thank you, my dear," her dad said, taking a little bow. Then he scooped the lumpy concoction onto plates while his wife, brandishing her dullest knife, hacked thick slices off the meatbrain.

The meat turned out to be tough and gray all the way through, but Gladys thought that was at least better than it being raw. She forced herself to eat a few bland, chewy bites. The mashed puffs, despite their unappetizing form, didn't taste that bad—or at least the parts that weren't touching the scary gravy didn't—so she managed to eat a bit more of those. Sandy, meanwhile, moved things around so expertly and squirted so much ketchup over the whole mess that in the end it was impossible to tell whether he'd eaten anything at all. Gladys made a mental note to ask him for tips on his techniques.

Thankfully, Gladys's parents didn't decide to do anything "creative" with the apples they passed around for dessert, and Gladys and Sandy both crunched hungrily on them. When they heard Sandy's mom's car pull in, Gladys walked Sandy to the front door.

"Good job surviving," she said in a low voice. "Did you even try one bite of the main course?"

Sandy gave her a look of mock outrage. "What do you mean? I *demolished* that brain!"

But his stomach betrayed him with a loud growl. They both giggled.

"You'd better get home so your mom can make you a sandwich. And maybe next time you'll pay attention when I try to warn you about the food here," Gladys teased as she passed Sandy his coat. "I mean, how many bad reviews does it take?"

Sandy shrugged. "Hey, what you think sounds gross, someone else might think sounds cool. Or vice versa."

Gladys thought about her dinner at Parm's house—about how the Indian food she loved revolted her friend. "I guess you have a point."

Sandy took a final bite out of his apple, which he'd carried to the door with him. "You jusht gotta write whatshu wanna write," he continued through a full mouth, "and not worry sho mush about what uvver people fink." Then he shot her a red-apple-peel-flecked grin, pushed open the screen door, and bounded across the lawn.

Gladys found herself nodding as she turned to climb the stairs back up to her parents' office. Sandy was right, of course—and in a way, he was saying the same thing Ms. Quincy had.

She had a lot of rewriting to do.

# Chapter 10

# MS. QUINCY'S CUP OF TEA

THAT FRIDAY MORNING WAS SUNNIER than usual, and when Gladys finished locking her bike to the rack at school, she noticed a group of sixth-grade girls clustered outside on the steps. A very high brown ponytail was visible over a sea of fuzzy hats and earmuffs. Every few seconds, the group burst into giggles.

Gladys's heart sank. Was Charissa making fun of people this early in the morning?

Gladys would have preferred to avoid the group altogether, but they were blocking the only entrance to the building. Taking a deep breath, she climbed the steps as quickly as she could, bracing for an explosion of laughter as soon as the girls saw her.

But, to her surprise, it seemed like no one even noticed her.

Charissa's loud voice was carrying over the crowd, and as Gladys reached the top of the stairs, she couldn't help but listen. "Sure, it's two months away," Charissa was saying, "but turning twelve is a big deal. I don't want to just have a regular party with balloons and games and stuff. Those things are for little kids."

A murmur of agreement passed through the crowd. Gladys noticed that Marina Trillesby was nodding especially hard, even though just yesterday she'd been bragging about all the games she won at her cousin's sleepover.

"I'm going to have an *adult* party," Charissa continued. "My parents are setting the whole thing up!"

A few of the girls let out squeals of excitement, but Charissa just flicked her ponytail casually over her shoulder.

"What are you gonna do?" asked Rolanda eagerly.

"Oh, you'll hear about it soon enough," Charissa said.

The bell rang, and the conversation was replaced by rustling coats and clomping boots. Gladys pushed quickly through the door into the lobby and hurried down the hallway to class. She couldn't care less about Charissa's birthday plans, but it was nice to start the day without being made fun of immediately as she had dreaded. She entered the classroom confidently, took her seat, and pulled her new essay out of her bag.

Gladys had stayed up late typing for two nights in a row and was pleased with the outcome. She only wished she could have printed her letter on nice, cream-colored paper like Ms. Quincy's, but her mother's pink-tinted stationery was all she'd been able to find. She could have asked for different paper, but then her parents might have wanted to read the essay, and Gladys knew they wouldn't be happy with her new topic. She could only hope they would take it better if she showed it to them already printed up in the newspaper as the winning entry.

Ms. Quincy entered the classroom as the bell rang and took a final swig from her travel mug. Gladys had caught a whiff from the mug one morning and been surprised to smell something fresh and grassy—not the bitterness of coffee. During her next visit to Mr. Eng's, she'd sniffed all of his jars until she found the matching aroma coming from one labeled GUNPOWDER GREEN TEA. She wondered whether Ms. Quincy had picked up a tea habit while she lived in China.

Ms. Quincy called the class to order, then began to move up and down the rows of desks, collecting the math homework. When she reached Gladys's desk,

Gladys handed her two sheets: the homework and her new essay.

The teacher smiled as she read the first few lines on the pink paper. "I'm excited to read the rest of this," she whispered to Gladys, and as she continued up the aisle, Gladys couldn't help but smile, too.

Ms. Quincy didn't mention the contest at school the next Monday, and her silence continued for days. Almost all of the kids in Gladys's class seemed antsy about it, although no one complained at the lunch table as loudly as Charissa.

Gladys wasn't usually a fan of Charissa's tactics, but she was glad when, on Wednesday, Charissa goaded Marti into asking the teacher when they would get the results. But Ms. Quincy just smiled maddeningly and told Marti that the class would have to be patient.

The news finally came after science class that Friday afternoon. But, of course, Ms. Quincy didn't make the announcement in a conventional way. She didn't give any hint as to who the author was, but simply said, "And now I would like to read you our class's official entry for the *New York Standard* Student Essay Contest."

She picked a piece of paper up off her desk.

The paper was pink.

Gladys's heart stood still in the second that her

teacher cleared her throat, but when she heard the first line—"Dear Sir or Madam,"—her heart started pounding again. She'd hoped to be chosen as the class representative, but she definitely wasn't prepared for this moment.

"I am writing to tell you about my plans," Ms. Quincy read, "to become a restaurant critic for the *New York Standard*. You probably haven't heard of me before, but that's because I've spent the last four years in the little town of East Dumpsford, teaching myself how to cook. I'm an experienced writer, too, and I love writing about delectable dishes—but I'm also not afraid to be honest when food is disgusting."

The class giggled at this line, and Gladys's heart continued to pound. Ms. Quincy read on, through the paragraph about how Gladys enjoyed all kinds of foreign cuisines, and then about how much she loved to write about food.

"When I was seven, I started reviewing every meal I ate in a journal so I wouldn't forget any of them. There were delicious ones, like tender duck breast swimming in a lake of tea-infused gravy, with a side of slender asparagus stalks dipping their tips in at the shore. Unfortunately, there were less delicious ones, too . . ."

As Ms. Quincy launched into the essay's final paragraph, Gladys used her last few moments of anonymity to glance around the classroom. Most of the other students were focused on the teacher—Gladys even saw one or two of them smiling. Charissa was the only one with a sneer on her face.

Ms. Quincy paused before reading the last line and laid the paper back down on her desk.

"Sincerely, Gladys Gatsby."

Then she turned toward Gladys and began to applaud. To Gladys's surprise, the rest of the class joined in. She felt herself blushing and unable to look at anything but the top of her desk.

The bell rang shortly after, and when Gladys finally looked up from packing her things, several of her classmates were standing around her.

"Good essay, Gladys!" said Jesse Wall.

"Yeah," said Leah Klein, "I didn't know you were such a good writer!"

"I didn't know you were such a good *cook*!" said Peter Yang.

"I didn't even know you were in our class!" said Nicky McDonald.

Gladys murmured "Thank you" and slipped past the group as quickly as she could. But out in the hallway it didn't get much better, as Parm Singh and Marina Trillesby came running up to her. "Hey, I heard you won the essay contest for your class!" Marina proclaimed loudly, causing several heads to turn in their direction.

"Nice job," Parm said. "Karen Newcombe won for ours."

"Oh, cool" was all Gladys could manage to reply.

The crowd around them pushed toward the front doors, and through the glass Gladys saw Charissa, Rolanda, and Marti standing on the front steps. Charissa had her arms crossed and looked like she had swallowed a bug. As Gladys let herself be swept out the door, she heard Rolanda saying, "It's just a stupid contest. I'm sure everyone will forget all about her by next week."

"Yeah," Marti chimed in. "Besides, you're still the prettiest girl in the class."

"Well, *that's* true," Charissa said haughtily, and she started to say something else, but by then Gladys was walking quickly to the bike rack, trying to disappear as soon as possible. The chance to achieve worldwide fame in the *New York Standard* was one thing, but being well-known at East Dumpsford Elementary might be more than she could handle.

Chapter 11

# EVERYONE WANTS A PIECE OF GLADYS

OVER THE WEEKEND, GLADYS CONVINCED herself that Rolanda must be right—in a few days, no one in Ms. Quincy's class would remember her essay. But when she walked into school that Monday, the strangest thing happened.

Someone said hello to her.

It was Joanna Rodriguez. "How was your weekend?" Joanna asked with a smile. Gladys glanced over her shoulder, but there was no one else Joanna might have been talking to.

"I had to have Sunday dinner with my grandparents," Joanna continued, falling into step beside Gladys. "My *abuelita* made her carne asada, but she *always* cooks the meat for too long, so it comes out all dry. It's, like, *too* asada, you know? But if any-one told her that, they'd get disowned by the family." Joanna sighed and tucked a curly lock of hair behind her ear.

"Your essay gave me an idea, though," she went on. "Maybe I could write an anonymous review of her cooking! I could type it up and leave it in her mailbox."

"But wouldn't she guess it was from you?" Gladys asked.

"Nah," Joanna said. "I've got, like, fourteen cousins—it could be from any one of us! So hey, if I write a draft, could you maybe look at it for me?" She shot Gladys a hopeful smile. "I want to make sure the description of the meat is really nasty, like that super-gristly steak you wrote about in your essay."

"Um, sure," Gladys said.

Gladys thought this request had to be a fluke—but somehow, all week, she found herself having similar conversations. During their break between math and social studies the next day, Ethan Slezak scooted his chair up to hers.

"So, Gladys," he said, "my church is having a pot-luck this weekend, and my dad always makes this boring onion dip. The last time I complained about it, he was like, 'Then make your own dip, kid!' So, um . . . I said I would." Ethan shook his head, like he'd never made a more stupid promise. "Got any ideas?"

"Sure!" Gladys said, and before she knew it she'd written him out a recipe for homemade hummus.

Then on Thursday, Gladys was just getting settled in across from Parm at the lunch table when Leah Klein grabbed the seat to her left. "Hey, Gladys!" she said brightly. "What have you got for lunch today?"

Gladys pulled her sandwich out to check. "Looks like some kind of meat with mustard on white," she said with a sigh. Then, in an effort to be friendly, she asked, "How about you?"

"Um, I've got this fancy cheese my mom bought—it's called Brie, I think?—on this really crusty bread . . ." Gladys's mouth watered as Leah pulled a long, thin section of baguette out of her bag. "But she put fig jam on it *again*."

"I'll trade you!" The words were out of Gladys's mouth before she even had a chance to think.

"Really?" Leah said. She looked as if Gladys had offered to do her homework for the rest of the year. "No one ever wants to trade with me. But after I heard your essay I thought, well, maybe Gladys might . . ."

It was the best lunch Gladys had eaten in a long time. She would have written a rave review of the sandwich during recess, too, if the other kids hadn't come up to her spot at the fence to talk to her.

"Hey, Gladys, how come my mom's cupcakes always fall apart?" Mira Winters demanded.

"She's probably mixing the batter too much," Gladys answered.

"Gladys, the pears my dad packs in my lunches are always so hard," complained Peter Yang.

"Make sure he lets them ripen on the counter until the stem area gets dented when he pushes it in," Gladys advised.

"Yo, Gladys, what's the best restaurant in town to take a girl to on a date?" Owen Green asked.

Gladys was stumped by that one. If East Dumpsford had a romantic restaurant, she'd never been there.

"Oh, shut up, Owen," Parm said. She flicked the sleeve of his Dumpsford Dribblers jacket like he was an overgrown fly. "No girl would ever go on a date with *you*."

"Parm flicked *Ow*-en!" Mira chanted in a singsong voice as giggles moved through the crowd. Owen and Parm both glared at her, though Gladys thought she saw a tiny smile cross Owen's lips before he loped off toward the swing sets.

This pattern continued over the next couple of weeks, until it seemed like the only people who hadn't approached Gladys for cooking advice were Charissa and her cronies.

"That's probably because they don't eat," Parm whispered as she and Gladys made their way out onto the playground one frigid afternoon. The far field had gotten too snowy for soccer, so lately Parm had become Gladys's "assistant," organizing her question-ers into a straight line and turning them away ten minutes before the end of recess so Gladys still had time to write in her journal.

Gladys followed Parm's gaze to where Charissa stood, scowling by the seesaw with Rolanda and Marti at her flanks. She didn't want to be on that group's bad side. Who knew what kinds of desperate measures Charissa might be plotting to win back her popularity?

As it happened, Gladys didn't have to wait long to find out. The moment her usual queue formed by the fence, Rolanda and Marti scurried over and began whispering to all the girls. One by one, they peeled off the line and crossed the playground to the spot where Charissa was now climbing on top of a mound of pebbles. Curious about what was going on, the boys quickly followed until only Parm and Gladys were left by the fence.

The whipping wind carried Charissa's voice over to them. "Attention! Attention!" she cried. "I have a *very* important announcement to make about my awesome birthday party in March!"

"Ugh, what nerve," Parm hissed into Gladys's ear. "I bet she's only making such a big deal of this because she's jealous of the attention *you've* been getting."

"Yeah," Gladys agreed, but it was hard for her to muster up the level of indignation that Parm was showing. Honestly, she almost felt relieved to see the crowd migrate over to the other side of the yard. Having to talk to that many people every day was starting to make her feel like an empty coffee mug, with nothing but dregs left at the bottom.

"Well, at least the swings are open," Parm said. "Shall we?" Gladys nodded, and Charissa's voice faded as they hurried toward the empty swing set. A minute later they both kicked off, laughing as the wind pushed at their backs and lifted them higher.

*Charissa can keep the attention,* Gladys thought. It felt good to be free.

# Chapter 12

## THE THIRSTY INTERN

FIFTY MILES AWAY IN NEW YORK CITY, AN intern at a certain large newspaper was trying to break free from her obligations, too.

When Anastasia had shown up for work at the *New York Standard* office that morning, the first thing she saw was that the coffee machine near her desk was broken. But before she could sneak off to a kitchen on another floor, Carol Wilkins, the secretary who managed all interns, charged around the corner breathlessly.

"Anastasia!" she cried. "I've been looking all over for you! Come quickly, there's an important assignment we need your help on!"

★ ★ ★ ★

At the sound of these words, Anastasia tore her eyes away from the "Out of Order" sign on the coffee machine. An important assignment? Maybe this was the project she'd been waiting for, the project that would get one of the newspaper's editors to notice her. Maybe she would finally be sent to a City Hall press conference or a war-torn foreign country! Despite her sleepiness, Anastasia the Intern (and soon-to-be Reporter?) perked up as she followed Carol back to her desk.

"The *New York Standard* sponsors a statewide sixth-grade essay contest, and the entries have arrived," Carol began as she shimmied herself into her office chair. "They're completely disorganized, though, and the judging panel needs to have them by the end of today."

"Sixth-grade . . . essays?" Anastasia asked disappointedly.

"Yes!" Carol cried, and went on to explain that Anastasia must 1) go to the mail room immediately to collect the entries, 2) organize all of the entry titles in a computer file, 3) make three photocopies of each entry, and 4) deliver the essays to the judges.

It was Anastasia's four least favorite tasks all rolled into one.

"Well, what are you waiting for?" Carol asked impatiently as she reached for the ringing phone on her desk. "Go!"

Twenty minutes later, after retrieving an enormous pile of envelopes from the mail room, Anastasia sat in her cubicle, holding her head up with one hand and typing slowly with the other. She only looked briefly at each essay as she logged it in on the computer. But halfway through this second tedious task, something caught her eye.

The essay currently at the top of the pile didn't look like an essay at all—it was typed on pink stationery rather than handwritten on lined paper like the others. In fact, it looked much more like a cover letter applying for the position of restaurant critic.

Anastasia sighed. This wasn't the first time the mail room had given her the wrong mail. She plucked the cover letter out of the pile of sixth-grade essays and stuck it on the other side of her desk. For a moment, she thought of looking through her recycling bin to see if she could root out the corresponding envelope. But just then Carol flew by the cubicle and, seeing the size of the pile still to be logged in, used one of the intern's least favorite expressions. "Chop chop, Anastasia, chop *chop!*" she cried, which sent Anastasia into another flurry of cataloging.

Anastasia worked at her computer right through lunch, then moved on to the copy room where, thankfully, the enormous copy machine seemed to be working properly for once. While the automatic feeder did most of the work, Anastasia thought about dashing off to another floor for coffee, but by now it was nearly three o'clock, and any coffee left would probably be cold.

Finally, the machine shuddered to a stop and it was time for Anastasia to deliver the materials to the three judges.

"Just leave the copies in the editors' mailboxes, and *don't* bother them," Carol said as Anastasia staggered by her desk holding her biggest pile of the day.

One of the contest judges was Wendell Pettit, editor of the newspaper's famous crossword puzzles. His office was in the basement, next to a shelf of enormous dictionaries. Another judge was Jean Sallow, a political columnist with an office on the building's fourteenth floor. Finally, there was Salome Mendez-Lopez, a news reporter on the City desk, which was located on the ground floor. Keeping this in mind, Anastasia stopped back by her cubicle for her hat and coat so she could leave the building immediately after delivering the final batch of essays. But as she slung her coat over her shoulder, she once again noticed the pink cover letter sitting on the edge of her desk.

*Protocol* was a word that Anastasia knew well, since it was everywhere in the interns' manual she had received on her first day at the *New York Standard*. Protocol was the series of steps that employees (including unpaid interns) were supposed to follow when faced with any number of unusual circumstances. If you found the coffee machine out of order, for instance, first you hung a sign on it that said OUT OF ORDER, then you went and told the nearest secretary, who then called Maintenance, who usually got around to fixing it after a week or two. Or if you were assigned to research a story for the newspaper in a town that was only accessible by elephant, the protocol was to rent the elephant first with your own money, then submit a form that listed your elephant rental expenses so you could be paid back after your story was published.

Anastasia had never used either of these two examples. Nevertheless, she was familiar with the protocol for finding a piece of mail clearly meant for one department mixed in with the mail of another. What she should have done was first taken the letter to her boss—Carol—to confirm that it really did not belong with the sixth-grade essays. Then she should have brought the letter back down to the mail room so it could be redirected.

But without her coffee, Anastasia didn't have the energy to make two extra stops. And she knew that once it was examined in the mail room, the letter would be rerouted to the Dining department—which happened to be located on the fourteenth floor, where she was heading now.

So, after delivering the first stack of essays to Jean Sallow, Anastasia stopped by the office of Fiona Inglethorpe, chief editor of the Dining section. The pink letter went straight into the editor's mailbox, and Anastasia the Intern went on her merry way, back to the elevator bank, down to Crosswords in the basement, up to the City section on the main floor, and out the building's front door.

## Chapter 13

# FOOD FIGHT!

GLADYS WOKE UP ON TUESDAY, FEBRUARY 26, with a stomach that felt full not of the creamy mushroom risotto she'd been dreaming about cooking, but of butter-flies. Today was the day that the *New York Standard* would publish its winning essay. Had her entry been good enough?

Gladys's mom had an early appoint-ment and spent the morning bustling around the house, searching for her briefcase and keys and hat. This was lucky, since it kept her from noticing how Gladys was hardly touching her bowl of Sugar O's. Even luckier, by the time she found everything she needed, she was running so late that she agreed

★ ★ ★ ★

to let Gladys ride her bike to school even though the streets were still slushy from a recent snowstorm.

"Be careful!" her mom shouted as she backed the car out of the driveway. Gladys finished strapping her watermelon-patterned helmet over her woolly blue hat and jumped on her bike, gripping its handle-bars through her thick mittens. The wind was strong against her face as she kicked off, but Gladys felt so happy to be riding that she hardly felt it. Would her luck hold throughout the day?

As she pedaled down the street, Gladys wished that her mother had left a little earlier—then she might have had time to make a detour to Mr. Eng's, pick up a warm croissant for breakfast, and sneak a look at the newspapers by the front counter. But since the streets were a mess, there were only enough minutes to ride to school.

Stomping the slush off her boots in the school lobby, Gladys wondered whether the teachers kept copies of the *New York Standard* in their staff room, or whether she could go to the computer lab at lunch to look at the newspaper's website. But it turned out not to matter. She had barely arrived at the door of her classroom when Ms. Quincy rose from looking at an open copy of the paper on her desk and beckoned Gladys back into the hallway.

The second bell rang, and kids rushed down the

hall. Ms. Quincy (who was wearing a pair of purple rubber boots that might have seemed weather-
appropriate until you noticed their frighteningly high
platform heels) stooped to talk to Gladys face-to-face.
Gladys saw her teacher's expression and knew that
her luck had run out.

"I'm sorry, Gladys," Ms. Quincy said. "But it looks
like you have not won the essay contest."

Gladys's face, which moments ago had felt so cold
in the icy winds, suddenly felt very warm. "Oh" was all
that she could say.

Ms. Quincy continued. "The winning essay was written by a boy—or perhaps a girl—from upstate named
Hamilton Herbertson. I've read it, and to be honest I'm
a bit surprised that the judges chose an essay about
*fighting zombies* in the future." She sniffed. "I thought
that your topic was much more original."

"Thanks," Gladys said, afraid that if she uttered
more than one syllable at a time her voice might crack.

"You did your best, and this class was proud to have
you as its representative." Ms. Quincy placed a hand
on Gladys's shoulder. "Are you going to be all right?"

"Yes," Gladys said.

"Good. Chin up then."

And that was that.

Gladys felt strangely empty for the rest of the
morning (though her lack of breakfast may have had

something to do with that, too). She didn't raise her hand during math or social studies, and thankfully Ms. Quincy didn't force her to participate.

At lunchtime, Parm tried to put things in perspective. "The odds were against you the whole time," she said as she poured milk over her Wheaty Squares. "Like I said from the start, it's just a game of numbers. And honestly, do you think those *New York Standard* people really read every single entry? They probably just picked one paper randomly from the pile and gave it the prize."

"Uh, thanks, Parm." Gladys took another bite of her sandwich. Leah and her gourmet lunch were absent today, so she was stuck with low-fat peanut butter and sugar-free jelly on white.

"Parm, you are such a *downer,*" Owen Green said, flicking a piece of lettuce across the table in Parm's direction. The boys' section of the table started just one seat away from Gladys, and apparently he was close enough to hear their conversation. "Just leave Gladys alone. If she wants to cry over losing the contest, let her cry."

Gladys swallowed her sandwich bite in a hurry. "I wasn't cry—"

"Oh, please," Parm countered. "I'm just explaining how the *real world* works. How it's full of *disappointment* and *heartache.* She's going to have to get used to it one day, and so are you."

Owen was pulling his sandwich apart, looking for more ammo. "I know how the real world works!" he muttered. "My grandparents live in the Bronx. Last week there was a shooting right down the block from their apartment. It doesn't get realer than that!"

"You think that's bad?" Parm scoffed. "Try going to India sometime! You should see what's down the street from where *my* grandma and grandpa live!"

Parm's hand was clenched into a fist around her spoon, and Owen was aiming a tomato slice in her direction, his flicking finger at the ready.

"Food fight!" Nicky McDonald squealed.

For a split second, time seemed to freeze—and then, all at once, the air over the sixth-grade lunch table was filled with flying food. Soggy vegetables soared out of Owen's sandwich in graceful arcs while milk-moistened Wheaty Squares shot off Parm's spoon like boulders from a catapult. Nicky launched baby-carrot missiles at Peter Yang, whose pear (perfectly ripe, Gladys was glad to see) splattered on the wall behind Nicky's head. Over at the other end of the table, Charissa and her cronies were shrieking and backing away from the melee, but some of the other girls were game. Joanna Rodriguez gleefully shouted "Snotbomb!" as she flung an open cup of green Jell-O at Marina Trillesby, who was quick to counter with a pudding cup of her own.

As her classmates' shrieks and the sharp whistles

of the lunch aides accosted her ears, Gladys felt all of the day's frustrations coming to a peak. She had not won the contest; she did not have five hundred dollars to pay off the fire damage or an award-winning essay to prove that she really was a good cook. All she had was this dreadful peanut butter and jelly sandwich, and the promise of many more to come.

Then, before she knew it, Gladys was on her feet, tearing the two halves of her sandwich apart and hurling them with all her might toward the wall on the other side of the room. The jellied half slid off immediately, but the peanut-buttered half stuck with a satisfying squelch.

The red-faced lunch aides closed in, and Gladys felt sorry for them—she didn't usually approve of cafeteria mayhem, especially when it involved wasting food. But just this once, as she admired the new peanut-buttery wall art she'd created, she had to admit that she felt a tiny bit good, too.

# Chapter 14

# PINK = DELICIOUS

OVER AT THE New York Standard OFFICES in Manhattan, editor Fiona Q. Inglethorpe was engaged in a food fight of her own.

At ten a.m., she had received a phone call from her head restaurant critic, Gilbert Gadfly.

"Iggleforpe!" his voice shrieked. "I burft my thung om hoth chocorip! I camp pashte emmyfing!"

"Mr. Gadfly, calm down," she said. "I can hardly understand you."

He did not calm down. "My thung ish scalgid!"

"Why don't you send me an e-mail, Mr. Gadfly?" she suggested. "Whatever the problem is, I'm sure that we can sort it out."

The e-mail that arrived in her inbox a few minutes later looked like this:

INGLETHORPE!

I HAVE SCALDED MY TONGUE DRINKING HOT CHOCOLATE FOR THAT WRETCHED CAFÉ CACAO REVIEW! THE AWFUL STUFF HAS BURNT ALL MY TASTE BUDS OFF! I CAN'T TASTE ANYTHING!!!

THE DOCTOR SAYS THAT IT COULD BE WEEKS BEFORE MY TONGUE IS WORKING PROPERLY AGAIN. I AM SO UPSET THAT I LITERALLY CANNOT SPEAK.

YOU'RE GOING TO HAVE TO FIND ANOTHER CRITIC TO DO THE REVIEWING. AND EVEN WHEN I'VE RECOVERED, I AM THROUGH WITH THESE MISERABLE DESSERT PLACES AND CAFÉS! I NEED TO SAVE MY POOR TASTE BUDS FOR ESSENTIAL FOODS, LIKE MEAT!!

NUMBLY YOURS,
GILBERT GADFLY

Fiona stared at the screen in disbelief. All caps— her biggest pet peeve. She fingered the fringe on the hot pink scarf around her throat with a sigh.

Fiona Inglethorpe loved the color pink. She wore at least one pink article of clothing every day, and it was not unusual to see her dressed in several shades of pink from head to toe. But what she called her "predilection for pink" didn't stop there.

She liked her ice cream pink (strawberries and cream was her favorite flavor), and her steaks had to be pink on the inside ("medium rare" was what she always told her waiters). Her signature pink pasta sauce (made with just the right amount of ripe red tomatoes and bright white cream) was the recipe that had first gotten her published in the *Standard*.

But that had been fifteen years ago. Since then, she'd reviewed eateries around New York City until her wardrobe became so well-known that maître d's and waiters recognized her and gave her special treatment—which isn't fair if you're there to write a review. So when she put her reviewing days behind her, there was only one thing left to do: become an editor.

Now, instead of eating pink foods all over the city, Fiona worked in an office. Her walls were gray. Her desk was gray. Gray sleet spattered against her fourteenth-story window. In the gray-walled cubicle just outside the door, her secretary's hair was turning gray.

Fiona typed an e-mail to the Human Resources department, asking them to post a job opening for a freelance restaurant critic. She had one more Gadfly review that she could print this week, but after that, she was in trouble. She could send the secondary critic out to cover next week's big steakhouse opening, but he already had a lot of other stories to work on. And maybe an intern could finish up the work on Café Cacao . . . but what about the week after next? She would definitely need more help.

Fiona clicked "Send" and turned back to the pile of papers on her desk that she needed to edit. But the black text on white paper looked so forbiddingly gray that she started to daydream about sneaking out of the office for lunch, even though it was barely ten thirty in the morning. She wondered how early her favorite Japanese restaurant started serving its bright pink salmon sushi. In fact, she was reaching under her desk to pull out her carnation-pink hat when her secretary walked in.

"Here's your mail," she said, dumping a new heap of papers on top of what was already there.

Fiona sank back into her seat. She'd been out of the office yesterday at a cheese convention, so now she had two days of mail to deal with on top of her editing. With a grunt of resignation, she began to sort through the pile.

It was all looking even grayer than usual when something unexpected caught her eye. Peeking out from underneath all the memos, letters, and articles was a pink piece of stationery. She pulled it free and saw that it was a cover letter—a letter applying for a restaurant critic position at the *Standard*.

*Wow, Human Resources works fast!* Fiona thought. It couldn't have been more than ten minutes since she'd sent them an e-mail. Maybe they already had this letter on file? If so, she was surprised that they had held on to a pink application; she knew that HR hated any deviation from the standard black and white.

*This one must be especially good,* she thought, *or they wouldn't have rushed it up to me.* And putting aside all thoughts of sushi, she read the letter with interest.

# Chapter 15

## FREE SAMPLES

GLADYS'S AFTERNOON HURRIED BY AS her class watched a nature video about the Amazon rain forest. Ms. Quincy occasionally paused the video to explain more about the Amazon's exceptionally damp climate—but if she noticed Nicky's pear-juice-dampened shirt or the glob of pudding moistening Joanna's hair, she didn't mention them.

When the final bell rang, Gladys grabbed her bag and headed straight to the bike rack. The food fight at lunchtime had cheered her some, but she was still feeling depressed about the contest. At least her mom wasn't picking her up, so she wouldn't have to answer the "How was school?" question right away.

★ ★ ★ ★

At home, Gladys wandered aimlessly from quiet room to quiet room. In her previous life as a secret chef, she would have cooked something to make herself feel better . . . but under her parents' new rules, she didn't think it was worth the risk. Having no better ideas, Gladys decided to do her "normal kid" thing for the day and play on the computer in her parents' office.

She clicked to check her e-mail first. Maybe Sandy had sent her a message—when she'd told him about her new DumpMail account, he'd been excited that they could chat online. But that didn't make much sense to Gladys, because they lived close enough to chat in person through their bedroom windows.

In any case, when she opened her inbox, there was one solitary e-mail waiting for her; not from Sandy, but from the address fi@nystandard.com. The subject header was "Your writing." Gladys's heart started beating a little faster—what was this?

Dear Ms. Gatsby,

I was quite impressed with the letter you sent me. I believe that a colorful new voice like yours may be just what the Dining section is looking for!

I was hoping that you could provide me with more details

about your professional food writing experience. Could you send along a few samples of your past restaurant reviews?

Cheers,
Fiona Inglethorpe
Chief Editor/Dining
*The New York Standard*

Gladys's mouth hung open—a position it didn't usually find itself in unless a big spoonful of something tasty was headed its way. Was Fiona Inglethorpe one of the contest judges? But if so, why was she calling Gladys's essay a letter?

The questions continued to pile up in Gladys's mind like layers on a cake. Had someone given Fiona Inglethorpe a copy of her essay? How else could *the* Fiona Inglethorpe, whose legendary recipes filled Gladys's dog-eared copy of *Cooking Pink for Pleasure*, have gotten Gladys's e-mail address?

The longer she thought about it, the more Gladys convinced herself that there were only two possible explanations for this strange e-mail: 1) She had been hit by a car on her way home, died, and was now going to become a writer for the *New York Standard* in heaven, or 2) this was a practical joke.

She didn't think that the first case was too likely, so she focused on the second. Maybe one of the kids at school sent it; she now knew firsthand how easy it was to create an e-mail account. Her top suspect was Charissa—she seemed like she would be good at forgery.

She knew one person who would be able to tell for sure.

To: rabbitboy@dumpmail.com
From: ggatsby@dumpmail.com
Subject: FWD: Your writing—Is this a prank?

Hi, Sandy.

I just got this e-mail, and I think it must be a prank. Maybe from someone at my school? Is there any way to find out who it's really from?

Thanks,
Gladys

Gladys frowned as she clicked "Send." She would almost rather be dead and a restaurant critic than alive and just the butt of a stupid joke.

A few minutes later, the phone next to the computer rang, startling her (she'd become mesmerized by an online video on how to make your own cream cheese). It was Sandy.

"Hey, Gatsby!" he said. "I got your e-mail. But then my mom kicked me off the computer—*as usual*—so I'll have to get back on later and check it out for you. Or maybe tomorrow. Anyway, it shouldn't be too hard."

"Thanks," Gladys said.

"So what else is new?"

For some reason, even though she hadn't wanted to talk about it earlier, Gladys felt okay telling Sandy about the disappointing contest results.

"ZOMBIES?!" Sandy cried angrily when he heard about the winning entry. "I mean, zombies are excellent, don't get me wrong—but I'm sure your essay was better. Who judged this contest, the aquituary writers?"

"Um, do you mean *obituary* writers?" Gladys asked.

"Yeah, the ones who write about dead guys. I mean, I could see why *they* would go for zombies, but . . ."

She had definitely found a sympathetic ear. In fact, Sandy seemed even angrier about the outcome than she was.

"Who is this Hamilton Herbertson?" he continued. "Did he write the essay as a joke?"

"It might be a she," Gladys said, "and I haven't even read the essay. Maybe it's very good."

"I doubt it!" Sandy muttered. "And if it is, I bet his parents wrote it for him."

When they hung up, Gladys was smiling for the first time that afternoon.

Gladys didn't hear from Sandy again that night. She fell asleep thinking about the mysterious e-mail, and when she woke up the next morning, it was the first thing to pop into her mind. Could anyone other than Charissa have written it?

During social studies, Gladys went through a mental list of all the other sixth-graders who might have pulled this prank. Nicky McDonald? No, his spelling was atrocious. Jake Wheeler? No, she sat next to him in computer class and he could barely type. Marti Astin? No, there was some truth to Charissa's accusation that Marti had never had an original idea in her life . . .

Gladys was so lost in thought that Ms. Quincy called her name to give an answer three times before she heard it. After that, Gladys tried to pay more attention, but it was hard not to slip back into examining her list. What about Mira Winters? No, Gladys had heard her say she didn't have Internet at home . . .

Gladys paid special attention to the conversations at the lunch table that day, but didn't hear anything about a prank, joke, or e-mail. Charissa continued to drop vague clues about her birthday plans, which kept most of the girls hanging on her every word. And at recess on the playground, no one said anything to Gladys at all—which was the perfectly normal state of things since Charissa had regained her most-popular-girl status. Perched atop the icy monkey bars, Gladys finally allowed herself to consider what had seemed impossible yesterday. Could the e-mail be *real*?

A cold drizzle was falling later that afternoon when Gladys got home from school. Once inside, she made a beeline for the computer, where she found two new messages in her Inbox. The first was another message from fi@nystandard.com, with that day's date and the subject "Your writing (follow-up)."

Dear Ms. Gatsby,

I attempted to reach you yesterday at this e-mail address, but received no reply, so I am trying again. I was hoping that you might be able to send me some samples of your professional restaurant criticism, since I am trying to assess whether you might be a candidate for future assignments with the Dining section.

Would you please let me know whether you have received my e-mails?

Cheers,
Fiona Inglethorpe
Chief Editor/Dining
*The New York Standard*

Gladys read this new e-mail, then reread it, her pulse pounding. If this was a joke, someone sure was putting in a lot of effort.

Too much effort. There was only one kid Gladys knew who would work this hard to make her writing sound adult and professional, and that was Gladys herself.

The second e-mail was from Sandy.

Hey Gladys,

Sorry this took so long but my mom just started this dumb new rule that I have to finish all my homework before I can go on the web.

Anyway I checked the servers that the e-mail was sent through and it looks real to me. I even did a search on the IP address and guess what, it belongs to "The New York Standard Company"! Crazy huh?

Sandy

So it wasn't a joke at all. Fiona Inglethorpe must have seen Gladys's essay and thought it was a *real* cover letter from a real adult writer. She even thought it was good enough to ask Gladys for more writing.

Gladys had been keeping one of the most important food editors in the world waiting more than twenty-four hours for a response!

Breathing fast now, Gladys clicked back to the original e-mail and began to type.

Dear Ms. Inglethorpe,

Thank you so much for e-mailing me. I'm sorry I didn't write back sooner. I've been very busy with

Here Gladys paused and tried to think of the right thing to say. Homework? No. Social studies? Definitely not. Finally, she settled on:

I've been very busy with other assignments.

Content with that, she hurried on.

I'll be happy to send you some samples of my professional restaurant reviews tomorrow. I hope that won't be too late!

Sincerely,
Gladys Gatsby

Gladys read the note over one more time—it wasn't great writing, but she had waited too long to respond to fuss over every word. It wasn't until after she clicked "Send" that she let herself slow down and think.

She'd just sent an e-mail to the chief editor of the Dining section of the *New York Standard,* promising to send in professional restaurant reviews. Professional reviews that didn't exist.

*Fudge,* she thought. What was she going to do now?

## Chapter 16

# KEEP AWAY FROM MOM AND POP'S KITCHEN!

GLADYS JUMPED AS A THUNDERCLAP sounded outside; the lights dimmed, and she heard the computer make a funny sound. The lights came back on full strength a moment later, but a message popped up on the screen saying that the Internet connection was lost.

Gladys turned off the computer and sat for a full ten minutes in front of the blank screen, working things out in her mind. She had promised to supply Fiona Inglethorpe with samples (plural!) of her restaurant reviews, meaning that she couldn't get away with sending less than two. But what restaurants could she write about? She couldn't remember the last time her parents had taken her out

★ ★ ★ ★

to eat somewhere new. And even if she could convince them to eat out tonight—which she highly doubted with this storm—she would still be one review short. She was going to have to write about places where she'd already eaten.

But where? The only restaurants Gladys had ever been to that seemed worth reviewing were the ones she'd visited in New York City with her aunt . . . and that was so long ago, she didn't even remember any of their names.

She would have to write about meals she had eaten more recently. But she ate so little of the food her parents brought home from places like Sticky Burger or Pathetti's Pies, she surely couldn't write about them . . . and according to Aunt Lydia, Sticky's and Pathetti's didn't even count as restaurants, anyway.

The best thing to do, Gladys decided, would be to look at the *New York Standard*'s most recent restaurant reviews for inspiration. And since the Internet was down and she couldn't look at the website, she would have to get her hands on a paper copy.

When she stepped out onto the front porch, the rain was coming down much harder than it had been on the way home from school. Suddenly her coat and boots seemed very flimsy, and she wondered how she would possibly make it to Mr. Eng's shop and back.

"Hey, Gladys!" a voice called. "Where're ya going?"

It was Sandy, standing on his front porch and

watching the rain. Happy to see him, Gladys ran over. "I have to go to Mr. Eng's," she said when she reached him. "I need a copy of the newspaper."

"Don't you get it delivered?" Sandy nodded at the blue plastic–encased lump sitting on the steps outside of the Gatsbys' front door.

"Not the *Dumpsford Township Intelligencer*," Gladys said with a shudder. That newspaper was so full of typos that she suspected reading it actually made you more stupid. Also, it didn't have a Dining section. "I need a copy of the *New York Standard*."

"Oh. Does this have something to do with that e-mail?"

"Yeah. I can tell you more about it later, but I'd better go so I can be back before my parents get home."

"In this rain?" Sandy asked. "Are you crazy?"

"Um, I think it's letting up . . ." Gladys said as bravely as she could, even though she thought nothing of the sort.

"Wait," said Sandy. "I think my mom gets the *New York Standard*."

"Really?" Gladys supposed it was possible. Sandy and his mom had moved to town after the article slamming the landfill was published; like Ms. Quincy, they probably didn't know that good East Dumpsfordians didn't read the *Standard*.

"Yeah, I'm pretty sure she does," Sandy said. "Do you want to come in and see?"

"Sure!" Gladys cried. At that moment, the front door opened to reveal Mrs. Anderson, wearing sweats and balancing her laptop in one hand.

"Gladys, what a nice surprise," she said as Gladys and Sandy shrugged out of their coats in the foyer.

"Hey, Mom," Sandy said. "Can we have today's *New York Standard*?"

Mrs. Anderson raised an eyebrow. "Should I get your pipe and slippers, too?"

"What?" said Sandy.

"Forget it," Mrs. Anderson said with a chuckle. "Just an old person's joke. So, what business do you two have with the Dusty Dame?"

"The dusty . . . *what*?" Sandy asked.

"That's a nickname some people use," his mother said, "for the *Standard*."

"Why?" Gladys asked. She had never heard the newspaper called that before.

"Oh, I guess it's because some people think the *Standard* is a little out of touch, like a dusty museum or a snooty old lady," Mrs. Anderson explained, leading Sandy and Gladys down the hall into the kitchen. "And I have to say, sometimes I agree. Take today's Dining section, for example—there's hardly a restaurant I could afford to eat at or a recipe I'd have time to make." Mrs. Anderson sighed and set the laptop on the breakfast bar. "Of course, it's not always like that," she added. "Some weeks the writing is brilliant. But things do seem to have slipped a bit lately . . ." She trailed off as she grabbed a bottle of milk from the refrigerator. "How about some hot chocolate, guys?"

"Yes, please!" said Sandy.

"Thank you," said Gladys. She stepped up on the footrest of one of the kitchen stools like she was climbing a ladder and hoisted herself into the high seat. A minute later, there was a pan of milk warming on the stove, and Mrs. Anderson was snapping a chocolate bar into pieces and measuring sugar out of a large white canister. Gladys had to smile—Mrs. Anderson might complain that the *Standard* recipes were too time-consuming, but she still made hot chocolate the old-fashioned way.

Mrs. Anderson reached up into the cupboard and took down three cups. "I think I'll have some, too," she said.

Sandy nudged Gladys and pointed to the end of the breakfast bar, where a thick, somewhat mangled-looking newspaper sat on top of a pile of mail.

"Oh, right, you wanted the paper," Mrs. Anderson said, sliding it down the bar toward them. "Don't tell me you both have current events projects to work on?"

"Yeah, current events," said Sandy. As soon as his mom was busy again, this time sprinkling spices into the pan, Sandy whispered, "So what's going on?"

"I need the Dining section," Gladys whispered back. She unfolded the newspaper and they turned the pages together, looking for the word *Dining*.

"Now, where am I supposed to put these?" Mrs. Anderson said, laughing. She maneuvered the two full mugs to either side of the wide newspaper pages. "Be careful not to spill on the articles you're going to use!"

Gladys was momentarily sidetracked by the scrumptious scents rising from her mug. She gave the surface a strong cooling blow, then took a sip of the velvety, sweet, and slightly spicy concoction. There was definitely some extra-fancy Vietnamese cinnamon in there! When she surfaced again, she saw that Sandy was turning the pages *back,* toward the beginning of the newspaper.

"What are you doing?" she hissed.

"I thought it might be easier to check the table of contents."

"Oh, yeah. Good idea."

"It's in section D," Sandy said, and immediately began to rifle through the different clusters of pages that made up the newspaper's sections. "B . . . C . . . E . . . F . . . huh?" Sandy started again, with Gladys leaning over to help. But it was no use—Section D was missing.

"Mrs. Anderson!" Gladys cried—perhaps a bit too urgently, because Sandy's mom spun around with her cup of hot chocolate and slopped a substantial amount onto her saucer.

"Yes, Gladys?" she replied, her eyes wide.

Gladys made an effort to bring her voice back to its normal volume. "Could I see the Dining section you were talking about before?"

"Today's Dining section?"

"Yes."

"I'm sorry," she said, "but I thought it was so worthless, I already used it to paper the rabbits' cage."

Gladys and Sandy exchanged a look of horror, leapt down from their stools, and tore down the hall toward the Rabbit Room.

Once inside, Sandy flung open the hutch door. Little Edward Hopper was more than happy to be set free and bounded out of the cage immediately. Fat, round Dennis Hopper, however, was in no hurry to move. He sat heavily on one corner of the fresh newspaper—the very page, Gladys saw as she leaned closer, that contained a restaurant review.

"I need that page!" Gladys cried, and both she and Sandy tugged. Dennis Hopper didn't seem to notice at first, but then gave a loud thump with one of his rear legs and took a small hop forward, settling himself squarely in the middle of the sheet Gladys and Sandy were pulling.

"Stupid rabbit," Sandy groaned, but then Gladys got an idea. She darted over to the rabbits' food bag and a moment later was sprinkling a few pellets into Dennis's bowl. Hearing the sound of the pellets,

Dennis hopped over and stuck his face in, freeing the sheet of newspaper. Sandy pulled it out in a flash.

"Tricking Dennis Hopper away from the food section with *food*," Sandy said. "That's genius!" And, brushing some fur, a few stray pieces of hay, and a rabbit dropping from the page, he handed it to Gladys.

"Thanks," she said.

"So that e-mail you sent me . . ." Sandy said. "It was for real? The *New York Standard* wants you to write for them?"

Gladys nodded. "This may sound a little crazy . . ." she started, and she told him all about the second e-mail and her need to come up with two sample "professional restaurant reviews" by tomorrow. "So I thought I should at least look at some real reviews that were already published in the *Standard,* and then . . . I don't really know. I haven't been to a good restaurant since I was a little kid. What am I going to write about?"

"I'm sure you'll think of something," Sandy said. "Maybe this one will give you an idea."

"That's what I was hoping," Gladys said. With a bit of renewed confidence, she flopped down into the beanbag chair to read "Hamburgers Most Haute—A Tour of Manhattan's Gastropub Scene," by Gilbert Gadfly. But before she even finished the first column, her new shell of confidence cracked like an egg.

Gilbert Gadfly's single article covered no fewer than *six* separate restaurants. What's more, he had apparently been to each restaurant several times, or at least brought a bunch of people with him, since he claimed to have tasted more dishes at each restaurant than one person would ever order.

"Well, that's that," she said, throwing the newspaper aside and sinking deeper into the beanbag chair. "You can give the paper back to Dennis Hopper. I quit."

"Why? Didn't it help?" Sandy asked.

"It's worse than I thought," Gladys said. "That critic must have tried ten different dishes at each restaurant before he wrote about them! How am I supposed to compete?"

Sandy paused to consider Gladys's dilemma. Then he said, "Well, did he *like* all of the restaurants he ate at?"

"No . . ." Gladys replied slowly. "He liked one, and said that three of them were 'hit-or-miss.' But he really hated the last two. He called the hamburgers at the Skewered Swine 'rotting lumps of bovine carcass.'"

Sandy made a face. "I don't even know what that means, but it sounds disgusting."

"Like my dad's hamburgers," Gladys said, remembering the terrible night two weeks ago when her father had stuck beef patties in the microwave.

"Well, there you go!" cried Sandy.

"What?"

"Think about all the awful meals your parents make you eat. You've already written lots of bad reviews of those in your journal."

"But my parents' kitchen isn't a restaurant!" she said. *If it were,* she thought, *it would have been shut down ages ago.*

"Yeah, but *she* doesn't know that!"

"Who?"

"That Fiona woman! She can't know about every restaurant in the whole world. You could just call it Mom and Pop's Kitchen or something. Write about that time your mom accidentally liquefied the broccoli and tried to pass it off as green sauce for the spaghetti."

Now Gladys's brain felt like a rotisserie chicken spinning on a spit. "You think I should *make up a restaurant?*"

"It's not like you'll need to make up the meals," Sandy said. "You've really eaten those. Just the name and the . . . ambulance and stuff."

"I think you mean the *ambiance,*" Gladys said.

"Sure," Sandy said. "So there's your bad review. You should probably write a good one, too. Hm. Can you write about your own cooking?"

Gladys shook her head—she knew immediately whose cooking she would praise. Sure, she had only eaten dinner at Parm's house that one time, but she had feasted on enough delicious dishes there to fill an entire review, no problem.

"I know just the place," Gladys said. "Thank you *so* much, Sandy! I think this might really work!"

# Chapter 17

# AWESOMELY NUTTY

THAT NIGHT AFTER DINNER (A PIECE OF fish that had been blackened beyond recognition on the outside but was still frozen on the inside), Gladys set to work. She pulled last year's journal out from its hiding place in her pajama drawer and found the entry from her dinner at the Singhs'. Then she took her red journal out of her backpack and flipped to the reviews of the most awful meals she'd eaten at home. She read all the entries over carefully, then turned to a blank page in her red journal and began to rewrite them.

Gladys finished the good review before her bedtime, but had to work on the bad one by flashlight after her parents made her turn out the light. When she finally

★ ★ ★ ★

wrote the last sentence—"If you like your meat cooked all the way through, you'll keep away from Mom and Pop's Kitchen!"—the hour shining in green on her alarm clock showed the latest time Gladys had ever stayed up until. She tucked her journal carefully under her pillow, rolled over, and fell asleep almost at once.

Waking up the next morning was hard, and the day didn't get much easier once Gladys got to school. At the beginning of the morning's lessons, she quickly realized that she'd forgotten to do her social studies homework in all the excitement of writing her reviews the night before. Her cheeks burned as Ms. Quincy walked up and down the aisle collecting everyone's worksheets, knowing that she wouldn't have one to hand in.

"Do you have a reason, Gladys?" the teacher asked quietly, kneeling down at her desk when Gladys mumbled that she hadn't done the worksheet. "A note from home?"

"No," said Gladys honestly. "I just forgot to do it."

"Well, I must say that I'm disappointed." Ms. Quincy's voice was a bit icier as she straightened up. "That will be a zero for today."

But Gladys had other things on her mind. For instance, how much time it would take to type up her reviews after school so she could send them before her parents came home. Yes, they had encouraged her to use the computer, but she was afraid that if they heard too much typing coming from the office—rather than the blasting noises of a computer game—they might get suspicious.

As the class lined up for lunch a couple of hours later, Gladys found herself standing right behind Charissa and Rolanda.

"Obviously, I won't be able to invite just *anyone*," Charissa was saying. "I mean, these things get expensive. Not that my parents couldn't afford it, but I think it's best to keep the celebration small. That way, the focus will really be on *me*."

"I thought we were best friends," Rolanda said, somewhat huffily.

"Yeah, well . . ." Charissa drawled, tossing her ponytail over her shoulder and almost whipping Gladys across the face, "you're *one* of my best friends . . ."

At that, Rolanda turned up her nose and marched off to stand with Marti, who was tying her shoe several spots back. Charissa turned to look after her with a shocked expression on her face. She obviously wasn't used to being walked away from. But in a second her expression was calm again and her eyes fell across Gladys.

"Gladys!" she cried a bit too loudly, like she was greeting a friend she hadn't seen in ages. Just then, Ms. Quincy herded the class into the hall and toward the cafeteria. Charissa hung back and fell into step with Gladys, sneaking glances at Rolanda and Marti to make sure they noticed who she was talking to. "Man, I can't believe old Ms. Q gave you a zero for forgetting your homework!" Charissa said brightly.

"Um, I guess," Gladys said with a shrug. Actually, she wasn't surprised at all—she knew that Ms. Quincy was strict about handing in assignments. What's more, she was sure that Charissa knew, too, since she had raised quite a fuss in class when she received her own zero the week before.

"I mean, sometimes we're just too busy to do all this homework," Charissa continued. "She doesn't understand that some of us have *lives* outside of school! I have dance on Tuesdays and horseback on Thursdays and sleepovers almost every weekend and what I really *want* to do is gymnastics . . ."

Gladys let Charissa prattle on until they reached the cafeteria, only half listening to what she said. She supposed she should feel grateful that the most popular girl in the grade was paying attention to her, but she knew it was just to get back at Rolanda. Gladys figured that they would part ways in the cafeteria, but when they arrived, Charissa grabbed her by the arm and steered her to the opposite end of the table from Rolanda and Marti.

"So," said Charissa as she nudged Gladys into the seat next to her, "what have you got for lunch today?"

Gladys had her typical white-bread sandwich, and scolded herself for letting Charissa drag her too far down the table to trade with Leah. The only other thing in Gladys's lunch bag was one of Mrs. Anderson's experimental brownies—caramel walnut this time— which Mrs. Anderson had wrapped in a paper towel and pressed upon her the night before. Gladys never had the heart to tell Mrs. Anderson that she didn't really like walnuts. This time, she took the brownie, hid it in her room, and snuck it into her bag that morning, hoping to trade it during lunch as well. Now it looked like she would be stuck with both.

"Ooh, is that a brownie?" Charissa asked. "My mom never packs me dessert. She doesn't want me to look fat in my leotard."

"Really?" Charissa was one of the skinniest girls in the grade; Gladys couldn't imagine her looking fat in anything. But she also couldn't imagine getting enough energy for the afternoon from the tiny salad Charissa was pulling out of her own lunch bag. "You want it?" Gladys said, holding out the brownie. Charissa took it right away, of course, without protesting, proposing a trade, or even saying thank you.

Gladys was in the process of unwrapping her sandwich when a shriek nearly made her fall out of her seat. Suddenly, every face at the table was looking at her—or was looking next to her, where Charissa held the brownie at arm's length. She was shaking.

*Oh, no,* Gladys thought. Mrs. Anderson was a great baker, but she sometimes got distracted. Had something fallen into the brownie batter—a coin, a paper clip, a (gulp) spider?

Whatever it was, Gladys knew at that moment that her social life—if it could be called one—in the East Dumpsford school system was over. She would forever be known as the girl who poisoned Charissa Bentley, and Charissa would *never* let something like this go. Gladys clutched her sandwich, trying to mentally prepare herself for the humiliation that was coming.

"Oh my *God,*" Charissa said, her eyes wide with disbelief. "This brownie . . . this brownie . . ."

The cafeteria table was dead silent; all eyes were on them. Gladys shivered, and her fingers felt weirdly greasy, though she didn't dare look down.

"This brownie is . . . AMAZING!!"

Gladys had squeezed her sandwich so hard that the mayonnaise had burst out of it all over her hands.

A few seats down, Gladys saw Parm do her usual Charissa-eye-roll, and slowly the table began to buzz again with conversation. Gladys reached into her lunch bag and groped for a napkin as Charissa continued to rave about the brownie—how moist it was, how awesomely nutty and insanely chocolaty, how it was exactly what she wanted for her birthday cake in March, etc., etc. "Where did you buy it?" she asked finally.

"I didn't," Gladys said. "My neighbor made it."

"Well, where did she buy the . . . you know, the stuff that went into it?"

"The ingredients?"

"Yeah, the *ingredients*." Charissa was starting to sound impatient.

"Well, she usually shops at Mr. Eng's Gourmet Grocery on Hamilton Str—" Gladys started, but Charissa cut her off.

"Great," she snapped, then filled her mouth with another bite of brownie. Gladys took this as a sign that the conversation was over, and bit carefully into her own (now half-exploded) lunch.

The mayonnaise grease was gone by the time Gladys sat down at the computer that afternoon. It took her about an hour to type up her sample reviews, the terrible one of "Mom and Pop's Kitchen" and the glowing one of "Singhs' Paradise" ("a delightful hole-in-the-wall whose buffet serves up the best of Indian cuisine . . . and if the prices were any lower, the food would be free!"). She attached them to an e-mail addressed to fi@nystandard.com and titled it "The samples you requested." Now all that remained was the short note to the editor. Gladys took a deep breath.

Dear Ms. Inglethorpe,

Here are the sample restaurant reviews you asked for. I hope that you enjoy reading them. I would love to write a restaurant review for the *New York Standard*.

Sincerely,
Gladys Gatsby

She couldn't think of anything else to say, and she didn't want to keep Ms. Inglethorpe waiting any longer. So, gripping the mouse to control the slight shaking of her hand, she clicked "Send."

The editor's response was waiting for Gladys when she arrived home from school the next day.

Gladys,

I can't tell you how much I laughed reading your review of Mom and Pop's Kitchen today. I pity you for having suffered through so many meals there, but I'm glad you did, because it really produced a hilarious review! And Singhs' Paradise sounds like paradise indeed. Is this restaurant still in business? It sounds like it might be worth a trip into the suburbs to try.

As you may have heard, our regular restaurant critic, Gilbert Gadfly, burned his taste buds in a terrible hot-chocolate-drinking accident, and I'm trying to distribute his workload to other critics while he recovers. I would like to send you to review Classy Cakes, chef Allison Sconestein-Alforno's new "dessert bistro" on 42nd Street in Manhattan. The restaurant opens on March 15, and you will need to submit your review by April 9.

Please write back at your earliest convenience to let me know if you'll accept the assignment.

Cheers,
Fiona Inglethorpe

This time, Gladys lost no time in replying.

Dear Ms. Inglethorpe,

I am so glad you liked my reviews and am thrilled to accept the assignment. As for Singhs' Paradise, I think that they are closed to the public at the moment, but I hope that the owners will open a new restaurant soon!

Sincerely,
Gladys Gatsby

She figured that this was not a huge lie—after all, it would be great if Parm's parents opened a restaurant, though perhaps in a slightly more adventurous town than East Dumpsford.

Gladys clicked "Send." Then she spun around in the office chair in glee like she'd seen people do in movies . . . and accidentally whacked the computer tower, knocking loose a cable and shutting the whole thing down. "Oops!" she said, and in her frenzy to re-attach the cable, she knocked over a cup full of her mother's favorite fuzzy monster pens, covering the desk in feathers and googly eyes. She quickly scooped the pens back into the cup and carefully backed out of the room, worried that her excitement might destroy the office if she stayed any longer. Then she darted down the hallway to yell for Sandy out the window and tell him the great news the old-fashioned way.

"Woo-hoo!" Sandy cried, pumping his fist in the air. "I knew you could do it, Gatsby!" They agreed to meet the next morning, which was Saturday, at Sandy's house to discuss everything in more detail.

Gladys felt so cheerful all the way through dinner (Chinese takeout, her parents' old standby for Friday nights) that she barely noticed how salty her wonton soup tasted or how stale the fortune cookies were. Later, in bed, she had trouble falling asleep since she couldn't stop picturing herself at Classy Cakes, nibbling on pastries and secretly taking notes in her journal for her review. The review that would be published for millions of people to read in the *New York Standard*!

# Chapter 18

## COOKING UP A PLAN

GLADYS WOKE UP THE NEXT MORNING still feeling excited. She tiptoed past her parents' bedroom and slipped into the office to log on to her DumpMail account. She needed to make sure the message was still there and that she hadn't dreamt the whole thing.

To her surprise, she found a new message waiting for her from a different e-mail address: hr@nystandard.com.

The e-mail was filled with all sorts of details about her assignment that Gladys hadn't thought of. For instance, there was a contract for her to print three copies of, sign, and return to the *New York Standard* by mail. It was eight pages long and written in very official-sounding language.

★ ★ ★ ★

There was another form to fill out with her address and Social Security number. And the biggest attachment of all was a document called "Protocol for Freelancers," which included detailed instructions for dealing with any number of situations that might come up while she was working on her story. Among the section titles, Gladys saw "Protocol for Interviews," "Protocol for the Purchase of Food," and "Protocol for the Rental of Transportation (i.e., cars, vans, rideable animals)."

A creak from next door told Gladys that her parents were getting up, so she hurriedly signed off. All through breakfast, she felt a knot forming in her stomach that had nothing to do with the nuked frozen waffles on her plate. Getting the assignment yesterday had been so exciting that it hardly seemed real, but today it was looking awfully . . . official.

When Gladys arrived in the Rabbit Room next door, Sandy did not make her feel better. "So, what's your plan?" he asked.

"My plan?"

"You know, for getting to that cake place! Are you going to sneak into the city?"

"I-I don't know," Gladys stammered. In all her visions last night, she was already at Classy Cakes; she hadn't given any thought to how she would get there.

"Well, you can't ride your bike. It's, like, fifty miles,"

he said. "You'll have to go on the train. Or ask your parents to drive you . . ."

"My parents can't know anything about this!" Gladys was pretty sure that reviewing a restaurant for the country's biggest newspaper would fall into the "Anything else adults do that kids normally don't" category on the Unapproved Activities list. "They'd never understand."

"Yeah," Sandy said, "but don't you think they're gonna figure things out when the review is published with your name on it?"

"They don't read the *New York Standard,*" Gladys said. "No one in this town does. Well, except for Mr. Eng, and I guess your mom."

"Okay, but doesn't your dad work in the city? Don't you think someone might show it to him?"

"Look, I can't worry about that now," Gladys snapped. "There won't *be* any review to show them if I don't figure out all these forms and things! I'm supposed to send in my Social Security number. What's my Social Security number?"

Gladys and Sandy spent the rest of the day tromping back and forth between the two houses on a treasure hunt for everything Gladys needed to mail out her forms. They found a card with her Social Security number in her baby book, which was stuffed in the living room bookcase among the photo albums.

They found envelopes (pink, of course) in her mother's drawers in the office, and after scouring both houses for stamps, they finally found some in Sandy's basement in a shoe box filled with old letters.

Finally convinced that all Gladys had left to do was actually print the forms, fill them out, and mail them, they made their way back to the Rabbit Room. Gladys would take care of the final steps after school on Monday, when she had the house to herself.

"Oh, good," Sandy said. "Now we can get back to the fun part—your plan of attack!"

It turned out that Sandy had a great head for planning attacks on unsuspecting dessert bistros.

"Do they have a website?" he asked.

"I'm not sure," Gladys admitted.

"Gatsby, you should know stuff like this," Sandy said, quickly typing the restaurant's name into a search engine. A moment later, they were on the home page. With a few clicks, Sandy came up with the opening hours, a map, and a photo gallery of the restaurant's posh-looking dining room.

"Okay, it's gonna be open afternoons and evenings every day but Tuesday. And it's in Midtown, which is good because that means you can walk there from Penn Station if you're taking the train. The prices are expensive and in the pictures it looks fancy, so you'll probably want to be dressed up when you go.

The official opening date is"—Sandy made a few more clicks—"two weeks from yesterday, so that means you'll have three weeks to visit before your review is due."

"Sandy, you're the best," Gladys said. "What would I do without you?"

"I'm sure you'd figure this stuff out on your own," he murmured, but she could see a little smile of pride creep across his face.

Sandy e-mailed Gladys the website so she could look at it whenever she needed to at home. By then it was dinnertime, so they promised to meet again soon to brainstorm ideas for getting Gladys into the city.

When the phone rang the next morning and her mother said it was for Gladys, she assumed it was Sandy, so she was surprised to hear a girl's voice on the other end of the line.

"Hey, Gladys, what's up?" the voice cried enthusiastically.

"Who is this?" Gladys asked.

"It's Charissa, silly!" the voice answered. "Listen, let's hang out at recess tomorrow after lunch, okay?"

Charissa's voice had such a tone of authority that Gladys didn't even feel like she'd been asked a question—the only option was to agree. "Um, okay."

"Great!" Charissa replied instantaneously. "I like to have these things planned in advance. Like my birthday," she continued. "I've been trying for *ages* to iron out the details, but parents can be *so* difficult sometimes."

*I know what you mean,* thought Gladys, though she suspected her parents were difficult in different ways than Charissa's.

Charissa chattered on for five more minutes about her birthday, talking so fast that Gladys could barely keep up—there were problems with the tickets, though tickets to what, Charissa didn't say. Apparently, Gladys was already supposed to know.

"Okay, well, great talking to you," said Charissa after a while. "I've gotta go. Oh, and wear a purple barrette in your hair tomorrow. I'm gonna wear one, and that way we'll match."

"I don't have a purple—" Gladys started, but Charissa had already hung up.

Gladys groaned. She hated barrettes and hadn't owned any since she was four years old.

The next morning was cold but sunny, so Gladys was allowed to ride her bike to school. She pedaled slowly and took her time locking the bike to the rack, trying to time her entrance to school exactly with the bell so Charissa wouldn't have a chance to come talk to her before class. Gladys didn't want to find out what price she would pay for ignoring Charissa's fashion advice.

But in the end, Charissa didn't talk to Gladys all

day. She, Rolanda, and Marti were all wearing matching purple barrettes, sat in their regular cluster at lunch, and headed out to the playground together at recess without so much as a backward glance toward Gladys. *Maybe they made up over the phone last night,* Gladys thought. She wasn't upset about being snubbed—in fact, she was relieved. Being Charissa's best buddy was very demanding, and Gladys already had enough on her plate!

After school, Gladys printed out the *New York Standard* forms and filled in all the blank spaces. She tried to read them over carefully, but half a page into the "Protocol" document, she gave up—there were just too many words she didn't understand. She was pretty sure that the word *freelance* meant that she was agreeing to work for free, so what else did she really need to know? She didn't care about the money; she was just excited to get published.

So the signed forms went into the corner mailbox, and Gladys devoted herself to homework until dinnertime. With spring break coming up, Ms. Quincy was starting to pile the work on. "If you want a vacation, you have to earn it!" she said daily to a chorus of groans.

The next afternoon, Sandy had band rehearsal and couldn't meet. The following night, he had to go to dinner with his grandparents, so he and Gladys weren't able to get together until Thursday to talk about the Classy Cakes plan of attack. Gladys wanted to bring some ideas to the Rabbit Room, but she'd been so busy with homework that she barely had an extra minute to think. Even now, as she sat with Sandy and the Hoppers, her mind was half-occupied with her science lab report due tomorrow.

"Do you have any ideas?" Sandy asked Gladys.

"Nope. Do you?"

"Nope."

Gladys turned to the rabbits sitting on the rug, but they stared back at her as if to say, *We don't have any ideas, either.*

Sandy was fiddling with a Lego man he'd found on the floor. "Look," he said, "I've been thinking about it and . . . maybe we need to ask an adult for help."

"No," Gladys said forcefully. "No adults."

"I don't mean your parents," he said quickly. "But . . . what about your teacher? She's the one who got you to write that letter in the first place, right? Don't you think she'd be excited if you told her that the *Standard* hired you?"

Gladys shook her head. "Ms. Quincy's always calling up the parents of kids who misbehave in class. School rules probably say she *has* to tell your parents if you're up to something strange."

Sandy twisted the Lego man's head off thoughtfully, then stuck it back on again. "Okay," he said. "Then what about my mom? She's really into cooking, and she really likes you. Plus, overall she's pretty cool . . . for a mom."

Sandy was right—Mrs. Anderson was cool. Gladys loved watching her glide around the kitchen as she fixed them snacks, and she was always happy to pull a cookbook off the shelf and show Gladys the recipe she'd followed. If she ever got kitchen privileges back, Gladys couldn't wait to try some of the techniques she saw Mrs. Anderson using.

But telling her about the *New York Standard* assignment was just too dangerous.

"Sandy, I'd love to tell her, really," Gladys said, digging her toe into the beanbag chair. "But you guys live *right* next door to us. Even if she agreed to keep it a secret, she talks to my parents sometimes—she could let something slip by accident."

"I guess you're right." Sandy flung the Lego man across the room. "But is there anyone else? Maybe someone who lives farther away?"

Gladys was about to say no again when it came to her. Of course! How had she not thought of this earlier?

"Actually, my aunt lives in Paris," she gushed, "and she used to live in the city. I'm sure she could help!"

"Great!" Sandy said. "Can you e-mail her?"

Gladys shook her head. "She doesn't do e-mail," she said. "But I could call her this weekend. I'd do it tonight except that Paris is six hours ahead of New York, so it's too late."

"Well, you'd better make sure your parents aren't home when you do it," Sandy said.

"Good point."

A few seconds later, Gladys heard her parents' car pulling in outside, so she stood up. "Hey, thanks for all the help," she told Sandy. "A grown-up writer can probably figure out all of this stuff on her own, huh?"

"A grown-up writer probably has a car, and doesn't have science labs to do and stuff," Sandy said. "And anyway, what are friends for?"

# Chapter 19

# A FRENCH CONNECTION

GLADYS DECIDED TO MAKE THE CALL that Saturday morning while her parents were off at a home improvement store, continuing their quest for the perfect new kitchen curtains. Sitting at the kitchen table, she tapped her aunt's long phone number into the receiver. With the time difference, it would be almost dinnertime in Paris, and Gladys hoped her aunt was at home rather than serving patrons at the café where she worked. In addition to ignoring the Internet, Aunt Lydia refused to carry a cell phone, so catching her at home was Gladys's only chance of speaking with her.

The *beep-beep* noise that the French telephone system used for ringing

★ ★ ★ ★

sounded once . . . twice . . . three times . . . four times. Gladys had almost convinced herself to give up when a voice gasped, *"Allô?"*

"Aunt Lydia!" Gladys cried. "You're home!"

There was a pause, then a sharp intake of breath on the other end of the line. "Is that my Gladiola?" Aunt Lydia cried. "Oh, hello, hello! Is everything all right?"

"Yes, everything's fine," Gladys answered. "I just wanted to talk to you."

"Well, of course! Let me just turn down the burner on these beans. I'm making this fabulous stew called cassoulet, but it has so many different ingredients that it takes just about all day to cook."

Gladys's stomach rumbled. She knew what cassoulet was—she'd seen recipes for it in *Tender Is the Meat* and Mrs. Anderson's *Larousse.* But it was just the kind of complicated dish that she'd never had enough time or money to make on her own. "It sounds delicious," she said. "I wish I could come over and help you cook."

"Oh, my Glamarylis, I wish that, too! You know I'd beg your parents to send you here for the summer if I thought there was any chance they'd say yes."

Gladys nodded, though Aunt Lydia couldn't see her. A summer of cooking with her aunt in Paris was probably the least normal-kid-like activity her parents could imagine.

"So, um, I have this problem," Gladys started, "and I was hoping that maybe you could help."

"Why, that's just what aunties are for!" Aunt Lydia cried with a laugh. "Lay it on me, my Glazalea."

"There's something I need to do in the city," Gladys started, "and I can't tell Mom and Dad. It's not something bad—just something they won't think is appropriate for a kid my age to be doing." Gladys paused, unsure if she should say any more. After all, her mother and Aunt Lydia *were* sisters, and she didn't want to put her aunt in the position where she might have to lie to her mom to cover things up. It was probably better if she didn't know all the details.

"Anyway, I know they won't give me permission to take the train on my own," she continued, "but they let me go with you when you were here. So I was wondering if, um . . . you might want to come visit? Like, sometime in the next two or three weeks?"

The phone's speaker made Aunt Lydia's long exhale sound like the rumbling of a garbage disposal. "Oh, I wish I could," she said, and sighed. "I truly, truly do. But right now I've only got about two hundred euros in my bank account. Do you know how much that is? Less than three hundred dollars. Even if I could get away from the café without losing my job, it wouldn't be enough for a plane ticket. I'm so sorry, my Glantana."

Gladys had known it was a long shot before she

even made the call, but still, a part of her had hoped. "Fudge," she whispered, trying to fight back the tears that were welling in her eyes. Now she really had no idea what to do.

"But," Aunt Lydia was saying, "maybe we can figure something else out!"

Relieved that her aunt couldn't see her, Gladys blinked hard and tried to get her voice under control. "Like what?"

"Well, this secret mission of yours—is it something that you really need to do all by yourself? Or could you pull it off with your parents around? You know, right under their noses without their figuring out what you're up to?"

Gladys tried to picture her family sitting at one of the delicate wrought iron tables in the picture on the Classy Cakes website. Her mom would be texting about work, and her dad's eyes would bug out when he saw the bill . . . but neither of them would pay much attention as Gladys scribbled tasting notes into her journal (which she could hide under a cloth napkin in her lap).

"Actually," Gladys said, "I think I could do it even if they were there with me."

"Then voilà!" Aunt Lydia cried. "You just have to trick them into taking you!"

"Yeah, but . . ." Gladys tried to think of some

scenario, any scenario, in which her parents would voluntarily take her to Manhattan. It had never happened before. "I don't think that would work. Mom never goes into the city."

"But your dad works in the city every day. Do you need both of them to take you?"

"I guess not—"

A hissing, popping sound sputtered out of the phone. "Oh, *mon dieu*, it's the cassoulet," her aunt said. "Hang on, my Glavender!"

Gladys thought some more while her aunt was away. Spring break was coming up. Could she convince her father to take her to the city with him one day? Probably not—he'd been complaining lately about how busy he was at work. But maybe, if the request didn't come from *her* . . . if it was something more official-sounding, like a school assignment . . .

There was a shuffling noise, and Aunt Lydia's voice came back. "Whew! Caught it before it overflowed. Now, where were we, my Gladragon?"

"Actually, I think I may have figured it out!" Gladys cried. "Our talk really helped. Thank you, Aunt Lydia!"

"Oh, anytime, anytime!" her aunt said. "You'll have to let me know how it all turns out."

"Okay, I'll let you get back to your cooking," Gladys said.

"Good luck, my Gladiconia! *Au revoir! À bientôt!*"

"*À bientôt,*" Gladys repeated, and hung up the phone. If she was able to pull off the plan that was brewing in her brain, she'd be having dessert at Classy Cakes in less than two weeks.

# Chapter 20

# EASY AS TIRAMISU

THAT FRIDAY, ON THE LAST DAY OF school before spring break, Ms. Quincy made an announcement.

"You've all done so well on your assignments lately," she said. "I know that I've been working you very hard. So I'm sure you'll be happy to hear that you have no homework over the holiday"—cheers erupted—"except for one very small project." The cheers died.

"It's a fun one, I promise!" Ms. Quincy continued, passing printouts with details down the rows of seats. "I would like for you to interview one of your parents, or some other adult in your life, and write a report about his or her job. And if you're not going away for spring break, you can get extra credit by spending a day at work with whomever you've interviewed. You've all written essays about your ideas for the future; now you can get some firsthand experience as well."

"A *report*?" Jake Wheeler groaned as he got his printout. "Aw, Ms. Quincy, why d'you have to torture us like this?"

Ms. Quincy smiled. "Actually, you have one of your classmates to thank for this assignment," she said. "I found it in my suggestion box!" Just then, the bell rang; she wished everyone a good week off, and class was dismissed.

In the hallway, all of the kids were grumbling—all of them except for Charissa, who shrieked as she wove in and out of the crowd. "*Who* put this idea in the nerd box? Who?? I demand to know! I *demand* that someone confess!"

"Fat chance," Gladys heard Owen Green mutter to Ethan Slezak, "unless they want Charissa to murder them right here in the hall."

Gladys pulled the straps on her lobster backpack tighter and scooted along the lockers to get past her classmates. She definitely wasn't in the mood to get murdered—not when her backpack finally held the assignment that was going to get her into the city!

Gladys's dad was a tax collector and her mom was a real estate agent. Her dad took a train to New

York City every day, where he worked in a large office building and often paid visits to other large office buildings to tell people how much money they owed the government. Her mom worked in a small office in East Dumpsford and often paid visits to small houses around town, where she tried to convince people that low ceilings were all the rage and that the smell in the basement was only temporary. Which job Gladys found *less* interesting was a toss-up, but when her parents came home that night, she knew immediately who she needed to talk to.

"So, Dad . . ." she said, slipping into the office where he was organizing some papers. "You usually travel all around the city for work, right?"

"That's right," he said.

"Do you ever work near, um, 42nd Street and Ninth Avenue?"

Her dad barely looked up from his papers. "Sure. Why?"

"Oh, no reason," she said quickly. "And you collect taxes, right? It must be really interesting."

He frowned. "I'll tell you what it is, Gladdy," he said, peering down at a spreadsheet. "It's not interesting, it's busy. April fifteenth is looming, but do you think everyone is going to pay their taxes on time? Of course not. I'm running around to five companies a day trying to get people to cough it up."

"Wow, five companies a day? That sounds exciting."

Her dad glanced up sourly, and Gladys quickly tried her hardest to look excited. "So I have this report to do for school where I'm supposed to go to work with a parent and write about it." She passed him the assignment description. "Do you think I could go with you to some of those companies?"

Her dad looked the paper over. "Your teacher wants you to come tax-collecting with me?"

"Yeah, can I?"

"Wouldn't you rather go to work with your mom?"

"No! I mean, um, I'm really interested in taxes," Gladys said in what she hoped was a convincing voice.

Her dad shook his head, chuckling. "That's just like you, isn't it? Always interested in the boring adult stuff. When I was your age, I would've thrown a fit if my father tried to drag me to the office." He made one last mark on one of his papers, then stuffed them all into his briefcase. "All right, sure. You can come in on Monday. But don't expect it to be fun." He rose from the swivel chair and started to walk out of the room.

"Well, maybe we can go for some dessert together after work?" Gladys asked. "You know, to make it more fun?"

Her dad turned back, looking at Gladys with what seemed like new respect. "Maybe there's a kid in you yet," he said. "Sure, as long as you behave yourself in my business meetings, I don't see why we can't get a treat after."

The alarm went off bright and early on Monday, March 18, and Gladys was prepared. She had her journal and a pencil for writing—for both taking notes at Classy Cakes and pretending to take notes on tax-collecting. She also had a map of Classy Cakes's location printed out from the website and stuck carefully inside the journal (though she hoped she'd memorized the map well enough that she wouldn't need it).

Remembering Sandy's advice that she should dress nicely, Gladys put on her best corduroy jumper, white tights, and the patent leather Mary Janes her mother had bought her for special occasions. Then, instead of her usual puffy coat and woolly blue hat, Gladys put on the stiff black peacoat she had gotten for Christmas from Grandma Rosa and the lilac beret that had come wrapped around a pepper grinder in her last birthday package from Aunt Lydia.

When she looked in the mirror, Gladys hardly recognized herself. *I'm not a sixth-grader today,* she thought. *I'm a professional journalist.*

Gladys's mom thought she looked so adorable that she insisted on taking pictures before Gladys left. She took one on the sofa and one by the front door, and was trying to convince Gladys to pose holding her father's briefcase when he pointed out that they were going to miss their train.

Gladys's dad usually walked to the train station in

the morning, but with Gladys along he decided it would be easier to get dropped off. Gladys's mom drove them to the platform and waved good-bye as they mounted the stairs. The wind was blowing hard, so as soon as they'd bought Gladys a ticket from the machine, they rushed to the little shelter halfway down the platform where most of the commuters were huddling.

"Gatsby," said a tall man once Gladys and her father had squeezed under the shelter.

"Robbins," Gladys's dad replied gruffly, and the two men nodded at each other.

"Who's this?" said the man called Robbins.

"Daughter, Gladys," said Gladys's dad. "Wanted to come to work today."

"Ah," said Mr. Robbins, and the two men continued to have a conversation using as few words as possible.

On the train, her dad let Gladys have the window seat while he read the *Dumpsford Township Intelligencer* and occasionally exchanged comments ("Those Knicks, eh?" "Embarrassing.") with Mr. Robbins across the aisle. Gladys looked out the window and pretended to be fascinated by the towns blurring by, but really she was going over the plan in her head and trying to keep her nerves under control.

The story she planned to tell her dad was that a friend from school had gone into the city with her parents and said she ate the best piece of key lime pie ever at a place called Classy Cakes on 42nd Street and

Ninth Avenue. Couldn't they go, too? Gladys knew that key lime was her dad's favorite, so she was hoping this part of the story would convince him.

The train pulled into Penn Station to a scene of chaos, unlike anything Gladys remembered from her midday arrival with her aunt. Men and women in business suits darted this way and that around the platform with grim expressions, clutching paper coffee cups and taking hurried bites from bagels or giant muffins.

"What's going on?" Gladys asked as they made their way down the aisle to exit the train.

"Rush hour!" her dad said, and offered Gladys his gloved hand. Even though she usually thought she was too old for holding hands, Gladys gripped it tightly as they stepped off the train and into the swirling mass of people.

Up an escalator, down a hallway, across a busy waiting room, through a turnstile, up a flight of stairs, and across a new platform, they stepped onto another train—a crowded subway train this time. There were no seats left, so Gladys's dad clung to a pole and Gladys clung to his other hand as the train lurched from station to station. Gladys determined that they were heading downtown from the descending street numbers, but then all the signs switched to street names instead. Finally, after she lost count of how many stops they'd made, her dad tugged her by the arm and they exited. They went through another turnstile, climbed some more stairs, and finally emerged into the sunlight.

"Where are we?" Gladys asked. She blinked as the light reflecting off the skyscrapers nearly blinded her.

"Wall Street," her dad told her. "Come on, this way."

Like the other men and women on the sidewalks around him, her dad walked fast, and Gladys struggled to keep up. Her Mary Janes pinched her feet, and she was starting to wish that she'd worn more comfortable shoes.

Finally, after walking through a maze of streets, they entered the lobby of a tall brown building. Gladys's dad flashed his badge at the security desk, then they rode a creaky elevator up to the twenty-eighth floor and exited into a huge room filled with rows and rows of desks separated by little walls.

"These are the cubicles," her dad said, guiding Gladys quickly around several corners. "And here's mine." He tossed his fedora onto his desk, and Gladys did the same with her beret.

They didn't stay at his office long; her dad just needed to check his work e-mail, drop off some papers, and pick up some new ones for that day's meetings around town. "You wouldn't believe which companies try to stiff us on their taxes!" he exclaimed as he led Gladys back out of the building. "Famous places, big names! Everyone's trying to get one over on the government.

Just wait until you see some of the businesses we have to visit today." Gladys nodded and hurried to keep pace with her dad as he sped down the street.

Their first stop was a building just a few blocks away, but much grander-looking than the building where Gladys's dad worked. Its outside was all shiny steel and glass, and the lobby had marble floors and a large pool with a bubbling fountain shaped like two golden lions in the center.

"Sackville Morganstern, can you believe it?" Gladys's father muttered. "I mean, if these guys can't afford to pay their taxes, who can?" Then he looked down at Gladys, as if he expected an answer.

"Right!" Gladys responded, perhaps a bit too forcefully. She had never heard of Sackville Morganstern in her life, but she thought she should at least try to sound interested.

Sackville Morganstern turned out to be some sort of huge bank. Once they received their visitors' badges, Gladys and her father were directed upstairs to a big room with a table, where they were joined by several more men and women in business suits.

All of the adults seemed delighted to meet Gladys, then equally delighted to completely forget about her as they spent the next two hours arguing over something that involved a lot of numbers. Gladys pretended to take notes in her journal at the beginning, but once it became clear that no one was paying attention to her, she stopped. It was probably the most boring two hours of her life, and if a young man that everyone referred to as the "intern" hadn't brought her a watery hot chocolate to sip, she would have surely fallen asleep.

At the end of the meeting, the head of the Sackville Morganstern group grumpily told Gladys's father that he would send the IRS a check. Then he called a security guard to escort the tax collector and his daughter out of the building.

"Well, that went pretty well!" Gladys's dad said as he led Gladys toward the subway entrance on the corner.

"Oh, yes," she replied. "Very good auditing, Dad."

They took the subway a few stops north to a neighborhood where her dad had a short appointment at the headquarters of a famous Italian fashion designer. "If they think that just because they're European they don't have to pay American taxes, they've got another think coming!" he announced as he and Gladys walked into the colonnaded building. This time, he left her downstairs in the designer's flagship store while he went up for his meeting. Gladys found herself staring at a mannequin in a low-cut dress that looked like it was made out of plastic wrap.

"Sorry, we don't carry children's sizes," said a haughty voice.

Gladys turned and saw a very skinny salesgirl standing next to her.

"That's okay," Gladys said. "I don't think it's really my style."

"Well, not everyone can wear Gianella," the salesgirl responded in a huff. "Our clientele is very exclusive. That's why we're the toast of Soho."

Soho . . . the neighborhood name made Gladys's mouth water. Why was that? Oh, yes—she had read a review of a delicious-sounding Middle Eastern restaurant in the *New York Standard* just a few months back.

"Are we near Salaam Soho?" Gladys blurted, just as the salesgirl began to step away. "I read that they make the most delicious pita bread in Manhattan."

The salesgirl looked blankly at Gladys for a moment, then shrugged a bony shoulder. "I haven't eaten carbs in two years," she said. "No one at Gianella does." And she walked off.

Gladys was relieved when her dad came back a few minutes later, fastening the clasp on his briefcase.

"Easy as pie," he said as they walked out of the shop.

"Or maybe you should say 'easy as tiramisu,'" Gladys suggested. "You know, because they're Italian?" Gladys got such a look of confusion from her dad that she decided to keep her food jokes to herself after that.

When they emerged from the subway again, this time near Central Park, the sun was high and people were streaming out of the surrounding buildings to find lunch. Gladys's dad bought them both hot dogs from a vendor, and they ate in a patch of sunlight at the park's edge. (*Not exactly gourmet,* Gladys scribbled in her journal after, *but surprisingly satisfying after a hard morning's work.* ★★✔) Then they crossed the street and climbed the stairs of a beautiful white building that looked like a palace.

A doorman in a black-and-gold uniform waved them into a lobby lined with oriental carpets and lit by sparkling chandeliers. "Would you believe that a fancy hotel like this is trying to avoid paying its taxes?" Gladys's father muttered with disgust.

"Unbelievable, Dad," said Gladys, who was starting to notice a pattern.

This meeting took place in a sumptuous office with a crackling fireplace. A tower of marzipan candies beautifully sculpted into the shapes of different animals sat on a large mahogany desk. But over the course of the next hour, the hotel's chief financial officer declined to offer Gladys's dad a check and declined to offer Gladys even one of the candies, causing both of them to storm out of the meeting in a rage.

"You'll be hearing from our attorneys!" Gladys's dad cried as the office's elaborately carved wooden doors swung shut behind them.

"You tell him, Dad!" Gladys cried with no less force.

Their fourth meeting of the day was another long one with another big group of people at *another* large table, this time on the forty-seventh floor of an accounting firm in Midtown. "Accountants! My own people! They should know better," Gladys's dad groaned as they returned their visitors' badges after. "Well, Gladdy, we've just got one meeting left. You've been a real trouper so far."

"What's our last stop?" Gladys asked as they emerged once again onto the city streets.

"It's not far," her father replied. "Just over at 40th Street and Eighth Avenue." Gladys's heart skipped a beat—that was only a few blocks away from Classy Cakes! It should be easy to convince him to swing by there after the meeting was over.

"You won't *believe* what company we're going to," her dad was saying. "The nerve of these bigwigs, thinking they're too important to pay their taxes on time . . ."

"Yeah, well, we'll show them!" Gladys chimed in. *And then,* she thought, *we'll taste cakes and pies, flans and profiteroles . . .*

Her mind was still happily occupied with desserts when they turned the corner onto Eighth Avenue and headed toward a towering gray skyscraper. But when they swept through the rotating glass doors, Gladys froze.

A sign hanging high over the gleaming lobby read:

WELCOME TO THE NEW YORK STANDARD BUILDING

# Chapter 21

# LIKE A PIE TO THE FACE

"THE NEW YORK STANDARD," GLADYS'S father announced, shaking his head gravely. "Those tax-evading scoundrels! Those money-plundering thieves!"

"Dad, keep your voice down!" Gladys begged, looking around. The lobby was full of people hurrying back and forth— what if someone who worked in the Dining section heard him?

"Why shouldn't the world know that the famous *Standard* thinks it's too good for taxes? It's not like they're going to print the story themselves!"

Gladys's mind was racing, but there was one thing she knew—she could not take another step toward the *New York*

★★★★

*Standard* offices. What if she ran into an editor? What if they asked her name? She couldn't lie about that in front of her father. She had to do something.

"Hey, Dad," Gladys said, trying to sound casual, "I think I'll just stay down here in the lobby for this one, like I did at Gianella."

"Don't be silly," he said. "This is my biggest case of the day! We'll shoot straight up to the twenty-sixth floor, and we'll really show them—you don't want to miss this!" He started toward the elevator bank.

But Gladys stayed where she was. It took her father several steps to realize that she wasn't beside him, and when he did, he looked back and gestured impatiently. "Come on, let's go!"

"Um, no thanks!" Gladys said, praying that her dad would get the hint and go on without her.

But with a grunt, he returned to his daughter's side. "Why on earth not?" he asked.

Desperately, Gladys tried to think. What would be an appropriately kid-like reason to refuse?

"I'm scared," she finally said.

"Scared?" her dad asked. "What is there to be scared of?"

"Heights!" Gladys cried. "I won't go all the way up to the twenty-sixth floor. Please don't make me!" She hoped that her tone sounded fretful enough.

Her dad gave her a puzzled look. "But you were just up on the forty-seventh floor at our last appointment," he said, "and you didn't seem scared then."

*Fudge,* Gladys thought.

"Um," she said quickly, "I guess it comes and goes?"

Her dad bent over to look her in the eye, and for a moment, Gladys thought that maybe she had succeeded in convincing him—until she saw the expression on his face.

"Now, Gladdy," he started. "Coming to work with me today was your idea. I thought that you should go to the office with your mom, but you were the one who said you were interested in learning about taxes. So let's not have any more silliness, okay? Auditing isn't for the faint of heart." And with that, he straightened up, grabbed Gladys's hand, and marched toward the elevators.

"N-no!" Gladys cried, pulling against his grip. "I won't go! *I won't!*" It was becoming less difficult to act hysterical, since she was starting to feel genuinely panicked. The situation was spinning out of control, just like that time last year when the lid slid off the popcorn she was popping on the stove. The kernels had exploded everywhere, and she couldn't wedge the top back onto the pot.

Her dad seemed bewildered now, too. "Don't make a scene," he hissed. Gladys looked around—people were starting to glance their way. Maybe if she embarrassed him enough, he would have to call off the entire appointment! Struggling with all her might to stay in place, she began to yank on her dad's arm in a sort of tug-of-war motion. But her feet, in their stupid patent leather shoes, continued to slide across the slick lobby floor toward the elevator doors.

"No, no, *no*, NO, *NO!*" she squealed over the *ding!* that sounded as the elevator doors opened. Gladys tried again to wrench her arm free, but instead her feet slid out from under her so she was almost lying on the floor—though her hand was still caught in her father's firm grip.

Shiny black and brown men's dress shoes shuffled by and high heels of many colors clicked around her as a crowd of people spilled out of the elevator.

Suddenly, a pair of stiletto-heeled pink boots skidded to a halt right in front of Gladys's face. Then, before she even had time to think, a strong arm grabbed her around her middle and hoisted her up off the floor and into the air.

It was in this way that Gladys found herself face-to-face with her editor—whom she recognized immediately from her picture on the back of *Cooking Pink for Pleasure*—while being carried by her father like a football.

"My goodness, would you watch that child, please?" Fiona Inglethorpe cried. "I could have put her eye out with my heel!"

"I'm terribly sorry, ma'am," Gladys's dad replied.

"This building is not a place for children!" Fiona

said, looking down to adjust the strap on her mauve purse, which had gotten knocked off her arm.

"I agree completely. Gladdy is much too old to be acting like this."

Fiona barely looked up and, dangling there in her father's arms, Gladys knew she had never been so happy to hear him use her silly nickname. Then, of course, he ruined the moment by giving Gladys an extra-firm squeeze and saying, "Now, tell this nice lady that you're sorry for getting in her way."

Gladys felt her face turning as red as if it had just been hit with a cherry pie. "I-I'm sorry," she mumbled quietly, staring at the floor.

"Well, I should hope so!" was Fiona's response. Purse fixed, she nodded quickly and turned to walk off toward the exit.

Everything felt like it was going in slow motion as Gladys's dad lowered her to the floor. *It's okay,* Gladys tried to tell herself, taking in gulps of air. *She didn't find out your name. You're safe.* But her cheeks still burned like she had stuck her head in an oven. That was not at all how she'd imagined her first meeting with the famous editor.

Then her dad said the only thing that could have made the situation worse: "With behavior like that, you can forget about dessert."

# Chapter 22

# A STICKY SITUATION

NO CAKE. NO COOKIES. NO PARFAIT.

*No FAIR,* Gladys thought bitterly as the train rumbled back toward East Dumpsford. She'd pleaded, and apologized, and behaved like a complete angel in her father's last meeting. But he'd stuck to his decision like caramel sauce . . . or shoofly pie . . . or some other dessert that should've been sticking to the roof of Gladys's mouth right now, but wasn't.

The city skyline faded fast outside the train window, and Gladys wished she had fought harder. Maybe if she had begged more, or cried, or promised to spend this summer at (shudder) Camp Bentley, her dad would have changed his mind. Then she would have been riding

★ ★ ★ ★

the train home with a belly full of sweets and a journal full of notes. Instead, her stomach and her pages were empty, and every jerk and shudder of the train took her farther away from Classy Cakes and any chance of completing her assignment.

Gladys's father dozed off, and Gladys sat in silence as the train stopped at Kew Gardens, Jamaica, Far Dumpsford. She'd been too nervous to notice much this morning, but now the smudged windows and sticky vinyl seats brought back memories of riding home with Aunt Lydia after a long day of eating delicious food around the city. What would her aunt say when Gladys told her that their plan hadn't worked?

Her dad let out a snore as the train pulled into Middle Dumpsford station, the last stop before theirs. Gladys watched as commuters shuffled toward the exits, and was seized with a crazy urge to join them. She could wait on the platform for the next train back to Manhattan, run the ten blocks from Penn Station to Classy Cakes, and get her review!

But her dad would be furious when he realized she was missing. Her parents would surely call the police. Plus, Gladys didn't have any money with her for train tickets or cakes. A bell rang, the exit doors slid shut, and the train lurched toward home.

Gladys spent most of the rest of spring break—when she wasn't writing the world's most boring report on tax-collecting—with Sandy in the Rabbit Room, trying to come up with new ideas for getting into the city. But every plan they thought up required her to sneak out of the house, cut school, or actually tell her parents about the assignment. Since Gladys wasn't willing to do any of those things, they were stuck.

"Hey, don't panic," Sandy told her after another useless brainstorming session the last night before school started. "You've still got two weeks. We'll think of something!"

But Gladys was panicking. Two weeks didn't sound like a lot of time.

At school the next day, she had even more trouble than usual concentrating, and when recess rolled around, she paced up and down the playground with worry. She was so consumed with her own thoughts that she hardly looked where she was going and walked smack into Parm.

"Ack, sorry!" Gladys said.

But Parm didn't seem to mind. "Hey, Gladys," she said. "Fancy meeting you here."

"What's up?" Gladys asked. "How come you're not playing soccer?"

"Oh, everyone else joined that mob," Parm said, gesturing to the far end of the playground. A huge crowd was gathered around—of course—Charissa Bentley. "I wish Charissa'd just pick someone already and get it over with."

"Pick someone for what?" Gladys asked.

"You know, the whole birthday thing."

"Oh." But then she realized that she still had no idea what Parm was talking about. "Wait," she said. "What *is* the whole birthday thing?"

Parm gave Gladys a look of mild incredulity. "Don't you know? She hasn't shut up about it for weeks."

Gladys racked her brain—she remembered Charissa talking about her birthday that time she had called Gladys on the phone, but she couldn't remember any details. "I guess I've gotten good at tuning her out," Gladys said.

"Well, you'll have to teach me your trick," said Parm, "because I've heard enough about it to last my whole life. Basically, the story is that her parents bought her tickets to some Broadway show for her birthday, and she gets to bring one friend. So, of course, everyone's bending over backward to be her best friend . . . except for us, of course."

"Ah," said Gladys. So that was why Charissa had that fight with Rolanda, and why the rest of the sixth-grade girls were following Charissa around even more than usual. Most other kids, Gladys mused, would try to have the biggest birthday party possible to show how popular they were . . . but only Charissa would think to pit all her friends against one another and make going to her birthday party the ultimate prize. You had to hand it to her: She really was a genius when it came to making sure she was always the center of attention.

"Well, she's got to pick someone soon; her birthday's, like, this weekend," Parm was saying. "I can't wait 'til it's over—the whole thing is so ridiculous, don't you think?"

Gladys was nodding in agreement when something clicked in her brain. "Did you say a Broadway show?" she asked. "Like, in New York City?"

"Well, duh," Parm said. "I'm pretty sure that's where Broadway is. Anyway, who cares? Look, we've got almost the whole playground to ourselves. Let's take advantage, huh?"

Normally, an empty playground and someone who actually wanted to spend recess with her would have made Gladys's day, but she had to find out more about this birthday trip.

"I'm sorry, Parm," she said, "but there's something important I need to do. I'll explain later!"

"Oh. Okay," Parm said. "Well maybe—"

But Gladys didn't hear the end of that sentence— she was already sprinting across the playground at top speed.

Charissa was standing on a mound of pebbles, taking questions from the crowd. She wore a purple coat and matching fuzzy earmuffs with the band stretched behind her head, under the base of her high ponytail. A quick glance around showed Gladys that several other girls were wearing earmuffs in this silly way, too. Joanna Rodriguez was even sweating, but she didn't take them off.

"Is it true that you're going to ride to the show in a stretch limo?" Leah Klein shouted.

Charissa let out a dramatic sigh. "I don't know *how* these ridiculous rumors get started," she said. "It's just a *normal* limo, not a *stretch* limo."

"Will the limo still be big?" called a voice from the back of the crowd.

Charissa laughed, and several of the girls closest to her quickly did the same. "Well *of course* it'll still be big," she said. "It's a limo!"

"Yeah, well, if it's so big," Marti Astin piped up, "shouldn't it have room for more than one of your friends?"

Based on the murmurs that rippled through the crowd, several others thought this was a fair point.

Mira Winters jumped to Charissa's aid and rounded on Marti. "She's only got four tickets to the show, stupid," she said. "One for her mom, one for her dad, one for herself, and one for me. Right, Charissa?" Mira gave Charissa a big wink.

Charissa's eyes narrowed shrewdly. "We'll see, Mira, we'll see. I haven't made any decisions yet. But it's true, there *are* only four tickets to the show. If there's extra space in the limo, we'll all just have to stretch out while we're watching TV." Another excited murmur went through the crowd. "Oh, yeah," Charissa drawled, "did I mention that the limo has a big-screen TV?"

Things went on like this for a while longer. Gladys learned that the seats at the Broadway show were "orchestra," which meant that they were very good, and that after the show the limo would take Charissa and her lucky friend anywhere in the city that they wanted to go. As the end of recess drew near, Charissa tossed her ponytail a final time and said, "Okay, enough questions. I've decided"—here everyone in the crowd seemed to take a deep breath at once—"not to make a decision until Friday." Everyone sighed in relief. "Meanwhile, if anyone has an early birthday present for me, they can leave it on my desk this week!"

The bell rang. Charissa hopped down from her mound of pebbles and headed for the school doors, the mob trailing desperately after her.

Gladys caught up with Parm as they entered the building. "Sorry I ran off," Gladys told her. "I just . . . needed to see for myself what all the fuss was about."

Parm still looked a little miffed, but she seemed to accept this explanation. "So, I guess you've heard the latest then," she said. "She's asking for presents now! What a nerve! What's she going to do, take the person who gives her the best present?"

"I hope so," Gladys said without thinking.

"What?"

"Oh, I mean . . . um, that's disgusting!"

Parm liked this answer much better. "Yeah!" she said. "*So* disgusting! Honestly . . ."

Parm kept talking until they parted ways for their separate classrooms, but Gladys's mind was only on one thing. She had to be the one who got the spot in that limo to New York City.

# Chapter 23

# NUTS FOR NUTS

AFTER SCHOOL THAT DAY, GLADYS RODE her bike straight to Mr. Eng's Gourmet Grocery, hoping that a good session of aisle-wandering would help her brainstorm. She needed the best possible present for Charissa if she wanted a chance at that trip into the city. But what could she get for the girl who already had everything?

The bell jangled overhead as Gladys pushed the shop door open.

"Gladys!" Mr. Eng cried. He was hunched over in the far left aisle, adjusting the temperature dial on the cheese fridge. There didn't appear to be any other customers in the store. Mr.

Eng gave the knob one final twist, then straightened up. "How nice to see you! Where's your friend?"

"You mean Sandy?" The last few times she'd been in the store, she'd come with the Andersons on their shopping trips. "He has karate on Mondays. I'm on my own today."

"Well, I'm on my own, too, as you can see." Mr. Eng's shoulders slumped a little as he glanced around at the empty aisles. Gladys knew that the shop didn't get nearly as many customers as the nearby Super Dump-Mart, but she had never seen it so quiet. The fruits and vegetables were as colorful as ever, but looked a little sad with no one picking through them, searching for the perfect spaghetti squash.

"So, how can I help you?" Mr. Eng asked. "Are you in the market for a snack? Or a new spice for your collection?"

Gladys looked down at the scuffed toes of her salmon sneakers. She wished she had money to spend in the shop; even if she couldn't buy ingredients for a cooking project, she could at least get a piece of exotic fruit or a fresh pastry from the bakery case. But her allowance was still being confiscated, and over break she and Sandy had decided that she'd better save the contents of her piggy bank for the bill at Classy Cakes, just in case she ever did figure out a way to get back there.

"Um, I don't actually need anything right now," she

said in a small voice. "I was hoping I could just . . . hang out for a while."

If Mr. Eng was disappointed in this answer, he didn't show it. A kind smile crossed his lips and his eyes crinkled happily. "Of course you can, Gladys. I'm always happy to have some company—especially when it's someone who appreciates fine food as much as you do."

Gladys couldn't help but smile back. "Thanks. So, hey, what exciting stuff do you have this week?"

Mr. Eng's eyes lit up. "Well, I've got a new Brie from Jouarre, a village in northern France," he started, "and a new shipment of baklava from Gaziantep—that's a city in Turkey known for its pistachios. And oh! I have something in the storeroom fridge that I think you'll like especially. Why don't you come on back?"

Gladys had never been invited into the storeroom before, and eagerly followed Mr. Eng's footsteps. Seeing what kinds of foods were waiting to hit the shelves would be like getting a glimpse of the future.

The storeroom was dimly lit and had shelves full of boxes as well as a large refrigerator. Through the clear glass door, Gladys noticed a display of several plastic cones with what looked like fuzzy green leaves blooming out of them.

"Basil!" she cried.

"Very good," said Mr. Eng. "This organic farm in California just started sending me samples of their herbs. They grow about ten different varieties of basil alone. Here, try this one." He opened the fridge door, snapped a leaf off one of the stems, and handed it to Gladys. She took a nibble. It tasted like pesto, like fresh thin-crusted pizza straight out of the oven, like summer.

"That's the sweet basil," Mr. Eng explained. "Now here's the Thai one." He snapped a leaf out of another cone and handed it to her. This one tasted different— spicier, somehow. Gladys thought of rice noodles, of soupy pink curry full of peanuts and potatoes.

Mr. Eng was about to snap a leaf off of a third variety when the shop door's bell sounded. "Another customer!" he exclaimed. "See, Gladys, you've brought me luck. I'd better go see if they need help, but you're welcome to stay back here and keep sampling."

Gladys nodded, eager to survey the rest of the storeroom's delights. "Oh, hello there," she heard Mr. Eng say from the shop. "Would you like your usual order today?"

"More than the usual, please."

Gladys froze, her hand halfway to her mouth with a sprig of something that smelled like rosemary. She knew that voice. The only thing that was odd was how polite it sounded. She'd never heard it utter the word *please* before.

Gladys crept toward the storeroom door to peek out. Her suspicions were confirmed: Charissa Bentley. She was fidgeting by the checkout counter, and even more strangely, she was alone—no mob of girls in sight.

"Of course," Mr. Eng was saying. "Now, I have a few different varieties this week: black walnuts from Missouri, butternut walnuts from Canada, and English walnuts, which, interestingly enough, don't come from England at all but from—"

"Whatever would be best in brownies," Charissa interrupted.

"Well, black walnuts are excellent for baking," said Mr. Eng. "Would you like to try a sample?"

Charissa's expression brightened at this suggestion. "Sure!"

Gladys watched as she followed Mr. Eng over to the nut bins. He scooped her a few nuts, and soon she was munching happily.

"Mmm, yes, these are definitely the best," she said.

"How much would you like?" Mr. Eng asked.

"Um . . ." Charissa swallowed. "I guess . . . about that much?" Mr. Eng kept a variety of containers stacked above the nut display, and Charissa was pointing to the biggest one.

"My dear," Mr. Eng began, "if I fill that container, it will weigh at least five pounds."

"So? It's what I want." Charissa was starting to sound more like her normal self now.

"Well, these nuts cost $16.99 a pound. So that would be an $85 order of walnuts."

Charissa shrugged. "Whatever. I can afford it."

Gladys couldn't see Mr. Eng's face from where she stood, but she imagined his bushy eyebrows sailing well over the rims of his glasses. "Very well, then, miss," he said. "Let me get that scooped for you."

Mr. Eng pulled a large container off the shelf and filled it while Charissa wandered around the shop. She spent an extra-long time at the pastry case before looking up when Mr. Eng cleared his throat. The container was about two-thirds full.

"This barrel is empty, so I'll have to get more from the storeroom," he said. Charissa shrugged and went back to contemplating the sweets.

Gladys scurried away from the storeroom door just as Mr. Eng came striding in. He whistled a cheery tune under his breath as he reached for a box from one of the higher shelves.

"Mr. Eng," Gladys said quietly. He jumped as if he'd forgotten she was there. "The baklava, from Turkey— you said it's full of pistachios, right? I bet she'll love it."

Mr. Eng glanced from the heavy box in his arms to Gladys to the storeroom door. "Oh, my customer? Do you know her?"

"Um," Gladys said, "sort of."

"But you don't want to come out and say hello?"

Gladys shook her head no.

"All right, I won't ask. The baklava, you said?" Mr. Eng shifted his grip on the heavy case of nuts and took a step toward the door. "Okay, I'll see if she's interested."

She was, especially after Mr. Eng sliced her a generous sample. In the end, Charissa bought a pound of the honey-soaked, nut-filled pastries, bringing her total at the checkout counter up to $92. The bell clanged as she staggered out of the store, balancing the baklava atop the bucket of walnuts in her arms. Gladys hoped Charissa's bike had a bigger basket than her own.

Mr. Eng was smiling and shaking his head when Gladys crept out from the storeroom. "Well, that'll keep the lights on for another week," he murmured. Gladys wasn't sure what he meant, but he certainly seemed happy. "So you know that girl?" he asked.

"Yeah, she goes to my school."

"She's been coming in for a few weeks now. Very bossy, but she spends an awful lot of money here, so I can't complain." Mr. Eng polished his glasses against his white apron. "Well, Gladys, I don't know how you knew she would like the baklava, but you were right. How can I thank you?"

And then, all at once, Gladys knew the perfect present to give Charissa.

"No need," she said quickly, zipping up her coat. "I just got the idea I came in for!"

# Chapter 24

# ALMOST-PERFECT PANCAKES

TEN MINUTES LATER, GLADYS RANG THE Andersons' doorbell. Sandy's mom appeared at the door.

"Oh, hello, Gladys," she said. She was wearing black yoga pants and had her hair tied back with a bright blue bandanna. "I'm sorry, but Sandy's still at karate."

"That's okay," Gladys said, breathless from her breakneck bike ride. "I was actually hoping to talk to you."

"To me?" Mrs. Anderson looked surprised, but pulled the door open wide anyway. "Well, come on in. What's on your mind?"

Gladys stepped into the house. "I was wondering," she said, "if maybe you could give me a baking lesson today. My,

★ ★ ★ ★

um, friend"—Gladys nearly choked on this word—"is having a birthday, and I want to make her something special. And since you're the best baker I know . . . well, I just thought I'd ask."

Gladys didn't like pretending that Charissa was her friend, but at least the part about Mrs. Anderson being the best baker she knew was true.

Mrs. Anderson smiled. "How flattering," she said. "Well, Gladys, I'd love to help out, but I've got to be at the studio in less than an hour to teach my class. So that doesn't really leave much time for a baking project."

"Oh," Gladys said, trying not to show her disappointment. It had been silly to assume that Mrs. Anderson would be able to drop everything to bake with her.

But Mrs. Anderson wasn't finished. "Hang on," she said. "There *is* one dessert I like to make that's pretty fast, because it doesn't require baking. Does your friend like nuts?"

"Oh, yes," Gladys said. "She definitely does!"

"Well, then, let's give this a try!"

Gleefully, Gladys followed Mrs. Anderson into the kitchen. Mrs. Anderson pulled a battered brown volume called *Street (and Dirt Road) Foods of the Malay Peninsula* from her cookbookcase and passed it to Gladys.

"The recipe's on page twenty-seven," Mrs. Anderson told her. She was already pulling ingredients out of the cupboard—flour, sugar, peanuts. "What do you think?"

Gladys turned to the page and found a picture of what looked like a pancake folded in half over some kind of filling. It might be risky to serve Charissa an exotic foreign dessert—Gladys had been thinking more along the lines of brownies or cupcakes. Then again, Charissa did just buy a pound of baklava. The heading for the recipe said *Apam Balik,* which small letters underneath translated as *Malaysian Peanut Pancake.* That might not be so bad.

"Trust me, if she likes nuts, she'll love this," Mrs. Anderson said, lifting the book out of Gladys's hands and propping it open against the toaster. "Now, we start by mixing a simple batter. Have you ever used a whisk?"

"Um . . ." Gladys wasn't sure how much of her cooking experience she wanted to reveal to Sandy's mom. "Once or twice," she said finally.

The next few minutes found Gladys whisking eggs, water, milk, and oil together in a large bowl, then adding flour, sugar, baking powder, and salt. Every time she caught Mrs. Anderson looking at her, she tried to mess up a little—hold the whisk at the wrong angle, or change direction midwhip so batter slopped over the side of the bowl. "Oops," she said, hoping that Mrs. Anderson was buying the amateur act. So far, it seemed to be working; twice Mrs. Anderson left her peanuts on the cutting board to come over and help Gladys get her technique right.

When the batter was ready, Mrs. Anderson heated a frying pan on the stovetop and splashed a little oil inside so the pancakes wouldn't stick.

"Ready?" she said, passing Gladys a ladle.

"Ready!" Gladys answered, and gently ladled a scoop of batter into the pan. It felt great to be cooking again.

"Wow, you really have a knack for this," Mrs. Anderson gushed. "It took me years to be able to make perfect circles like that."

*Fudge,* Gladys thought. She would make the next one less perfect.

Mrs. Anderson continued to talk as the pancake cooked. "This was my *favorite* snack when I traveled in Malaysia," she said.

"Wow, you've actually been to Malaysia?" Gladys said.

"Oh, yes, I backpacked all around Asia before Sandy was born," she said. "But I spent the most time in India, studying yoga."

India! Ever since Gladys had eaten at the Singhs' house, she'd dreamed of traveling there. She had about a hundred questions to ask, but just then Mrs. Anderson handed her a spatula and said "Okay, I think it's time to check whether the bottom's finished cooking." She winked. "I bet you know what to do."

The bottom of the pancake was a lovely golden

brown, so Mrs. Anderson dropped some bits of butter across the surface and spread a thick layer of peanuts and sugar on top. She instructed Gladys to fold the pancake in half with the spatula and press on it.

"Done!" Mrs. Anderson cried, and Gladys lifted the finished pancake out onto a waiting plate.

While she ladled more batter into the pan (in a much-less-perfectly-round shape this time), Mrs. Anderson sliced up the first pancake. "We'd better do a taste test," she said. "One of the most important rules about cooking is that you never want to serve something you haven't tasted yourself." She popped a strip of pancake into her mouth. "Plus," she said while chewing, "it's no fun to make something yummy if you don't get to eat it, too!"

Gladys tasted the pancake and thought it was delicious—the perfect combination of fluffy and crunchy, sweet and savory. But would Charissa like it?

On the next pancake, Gladys spread the butter and filling herself—"So you can tell your friend you made the whole thing!" said Mrs. Anderson—and wrapped the finished product in foil. Then she helped Mrs. Anderson wash the dishes and return *Street (and Dirt Road) Foods* to the shelf.

Once the kitchen was clean, they walked out of the house together, Gladys carrying her pancake and Mrs. Anderson shouldering her yoga bag. "Thank you so much," Gladys said.

"Oh, no problem, Gladys," Mrs. Anderson said. "It's fun to have someone to cook with. Sandy's not that interested, I'm afraid." She gave Gladys a wave as she jogged off to her car. "Let's do this again sometime!"

## Chapter 25

# THE PROOF IS IN THE (CARROT) PUDDING

BY THE TIME THE MORNING BELL RANG the next day, Charissa's desk was covered with brightly wrapped packages . . . and surrounded by girls eager to see her open their gifts.

"What is all this?" Ms. Quincy demanded as Charissa casually took her seat behind the mountain of presents.

"It's almost her birthday, Ms. Quincy!" Rolanda cried.

"*Almost* her birthday?"

Ms. Quincy was not a fan of classroom parties (she thought they took away too much learning time), but she grudgingly allowed small celebrations for students whose birthdays happened to fall on a school day. An almost-birthday, however, was entirely different.

Ms. Quincy disappeared behind her desk, and after a minute of banging and clanging her way through the metal drawers, marched down the aisle to Charissa and thrust a giant black trash bag at the almost-birthday girl.

"You can open those at home," she said. "Not on class time." And despite the moans and groans all around, she made Charissa load her gifts into the bag and stick it in the corner.

Gladys watched silently from across the room. So far, things were going even better than she hoped. She had predicted that everyone else would try to press their gifts on Charissa first thing in the morning, so she made sure to stay out of that fray. That way her offering would be more memorable.

At lunchtime, everyone else tried to sit as close to Charissa as possible, but Gladys took her regular seat far down the table, across from Parm. Still, she kept an eye on Charissa all through the meal, and when the last bite of salad disappeared into her mouth, Gladys jumped up. Her time had come.

She reached into the depths of her lunch bag and unearthed her small package, simply wrapped in foil. Then, breathing deeply to steady her nerves, she started up the table, package in hand.

Her target was chatting with her neighbor (Mira Winters today), but Gladys forced herself to butt in. "Charissa, this is for you," she said. "I thought you might like some dessert." She placed the package next to Charissa's lunch bag and slipped back down the table to her own seat.

Parm let out an exasperated sigh. "So now you're joining the race to be Charissa's best friend, too?"

What could Gladys say? She couldn't tell Parm about the *Standard* assignment—at least not right now in the middle of the cafeteria. But she also didn't want Parm—the closest person she had to a friend at school—to think badly of her. Gladys thought fast.

"It's not about Charissa," she whispered across the table, truthfully enough. "It's just that I love, um . . . Broadway shows!"

Parm's expression changed from disappointment to puzzlement. "You do?" she said.

Gladys couldn't blame Parm for being confused. The year before, the fifth grade had taken a class trip to see a Broadway show full of people singing about how miserable life used to be in France. Parm and Gladys had spent the entire bus ride back to East Dumpsford laughing about how silly the show was.

"Yeah, it's kind of a new passion," Gladys said.

"I had no idea," said Parm. "Well, maybe you should join Drama Club."

*With all the acting I've been doing lately,* Gladys thought to herself, *maybe I should!*

Meanwhile, the glances Gladys kept stealing up the table showed that Charissa was still talking to Mira as if nothing had happened. Had she even looked at the package? Gladys's spirits sank.

As the seconds ticked by, she found herself growing more and more angry. Parm was right—who did Charissa think she was? How dare she make everyone compete for her attention like this! Gladys ought to march down the table, snatch her dessert back, and tell that girl to stick her stupid limo—

Oh, wait, there was Charissa's left hand, starting to open the package.

Charissa's face never turned away from Mira's as she tore through the foil and lifted a rectangle of pancake into her mouth. She started to chew as she nodded at something Mira was saying . . . then the nodding stopped. But the chewing, Gladys could see, was still happening as Charissa turned her head away from her neighbor and toward the dessert in front of her. Slowly, as if in a trance, Charissa's hand reached for another piece. Then another.

Then Mira made the terrible mistake of poking Charissa on the shoulder and leaning over to whisper something in her ear.

"Shut UP!" Charissa snapped. "Can't you see I'm eating?"

Tears sprang into Mira's eyes; she pushed her chair back and dashed off in the direction of the bathroom. Charissa didn't notice—her attention was completely consumed by her dessert, and it stayed that way until every last piece of pancake was eaten, and every stray bit of peanut and sugar licked from the foil.

Finally, Charissa looked up. She wore the slightly muddled expression of someone who has just woken up from a long nap, or surfaced from a deep dive. She gazed around, taking stock of her surroundings. Finally, her eyes met Gladys's.

Gladys, of course, had been watching the whole time. Wondering, *Was my cooking good enough?*

Charissa beckoned Gladys over to the now-empty seat beside her, and, with an apologetic glance to Parm, Gladys made her way up the table once again. She had barely lowered herself onto the chair when Charissa started firing questions at her.

"What *was* that?"

"It's called apam balik—it's a Malaysian peanut pancake."

"Where did you get it?"

"I made it."

"You *made* it?"

"Yes."

"How did you learn to make it?"

"From my neighbor and a book."

"What else can you make?"

Just then, the bell rang. Lunch was over, and kids started shoving on their coats and streaming toward the door for recess. "Lots of things," Gladys answered with a smile as she and Charissa rose from their seats.

As their classmates made their way toward the exit, Gladys saw Parm step out of her line and hurry toward the bathroom. Gladys caught a glimpse of her expression, and it looked alarmingly like the one on Mira's face when she ran out of the cafeteria a few minutes ago.

*Fudge,* Gladys thought. Clearly, her story about loving the theater hadn't done the trick. In an instant, she ducked out of line, too.

"Parm?" she called as she pushed open the girls' room door. Muffled sobs were coming from the first stall on the right. She rushed over to the door and knocked gently. "Parm, can we talk?"

"Over here, Broadway Queen." Gladys whirled around and found herself face-to-face with Parm. Her eyes were dry and her expression didn't look very friendly. "That's Mira," Parm said, tilting her head toward the stall. "Anyway, what do you want?"

Gladys grabbed Parm's arm and pulled her toward the sinks. It was time to come clean. In a voice barely above a whisper, Gladys told her everything—about the e-mails from Fiona Inglethorpe, her failed attempt to get to Classy Cakes with her dad, and her desperate new plan to get a spot in Charissa's limo. By the time she finished, Parm's expression had gone from angry to surprised to concerned to amused.

"So *that's* why you've been acting so strange," she exclaimed in a low voice. "A review for the *New York Standard*! Wow. This is sort of a big deal."

"I know."

"I wish you had told me sooner. I might have been able to help!"

"Thanks," Gladys said, "but I think at this point I just need to stick to the plan I have and hope that it works."

"Well, it might," Parm said, but she looked doubtful. "What are you planning to feed her tomorrow?"

"I'm not sure yet," Gladys said. "I was thinking I'd just go back to my neighbor's after school and ask her to help me make something else."

"No," Parm said. "I have a better plan."

At that moment, the stall door at the end of the row creaked, and Mira stumbled out, glaring at them through red, puffy eyes.

"I've been waiting for you two nerdmuffins to get out of here for fifteen minutes." She sniffed. "Can't a person even cry in peace at this school?" She shoved past them to the sinks, washed her face quickly, and stormed out.

"Do you think she heard us?" Gladys asked nervously.

"No way," Parm said. "She only has ears for Charissa. Anyway, as I was saying, I have a much better plan. Tonight you'll come over to *my* house, and my father will teach you how to make gajar ka halwa."

"What's gajar ka halwa?" Gladys was intrigued.

"It's a traditional north Indian pudding made with carrots."

"Carrots?"

"Trust me, it's the best dessert on earth. My whole family goes gaga over it—every time we visit India, my cousins are asking my dad to make it *all* the time."

Gladys felt torn. On the one hand, she knew that the Singhs were wonderful cooks, and she didn't want to pass up the chance to learn how to make one of their signature dishes. But on the other hand, she'd already taken a leap of faith giving Charissa the Malaysian pancake. Would feeding her another foreign dessert—one made of vegetables—be too risky?

Parm was still talking. "My aunty and uncle in Delhi have a personal chef, but they *still* insist my dad make this for them. There's just something about the way he cooks the carrots and milk and raisins together that makes it extra delicious."

Parm had a faraway look in her eyes, and a smile on her face.

"Wait a minute," Gladys said. "Have *you* eaten this dessert?"

Parm glanced around to make sure no one else had come into the bathroom, then lowered her voice for good measure. "From time to time . . . yes, I have been known to eat a bowl of gajar ka halwa. Look, don't tell anyone, okay? If the other kids find out that there's a third thing I eat, I'll never hear the end of it. They'll probably all start trying to trade with me again—like, carrot sticks for my cereal or something." She shuddered with disgust.

But Gladys just smiled. If there was a dessert out there that Parm Singh would actually eat, it had to be amazing.

That afternoon, Gladys found herself grating carrots by hand in Parm's kitchen under the watchful eye of Mr. Singh, who had just come off a shift at his medical lab.

"I should have warned you that he wouldn't let us use the food processor," Parm said. Her father had set her up with a box grater and a bowl right next to Gladys's, but she had only grated one carrot so far compared to Gladys's four.

Mr. Singh chuckled, shaking his head. "A little manual labor won't kill you, Parminder. Do you want this halwa done fast, or done right?"

"Fast," Parm muttered.

"Besides, our food processor grates things too fine," Mr. Singh continued. "We don't want the carrot shreds to turn to mush as they cook."

Gladys finished grating her last carrot, and as soon as Mr. Singh turned his back, she snuck a few more out of Parm's pile to help.

When the carrots were ready, Mr. Singh heated up a lump of glistening butterfat called ghee in a large pan, then let Gladys and Parm take turns sautéing cashews, almonds, and golden raisins. When the raisins were plump and the nuts toasted, he instructed Gladys to scoop them out onto a separate plate, and Parm added the carrots to the pan. Then, after a few minutes of cooking, they poured in some milk.

"My recipe calls for a lot of nuts," Mr. Singh explained as the mixture bubbled on the stove. "Some people might say that's not traditional, but since the carrots get so soft, I like the contrast in texture that the nuts provide." Gladys was happy to hear this.

Once the carrots were cooked, Mr. Singh announced that it was time to add sugar and cardamom. Gladys knew about cardamom from Mr. Eng's spice wall, but it was very expensive and she had never cooked with it. Now, Mr. Singh showed her how to crush the black seeds with a mortar and pestle. Gladys didn't mind the work. As she smashed them, the seeds released a deliciously sweet and sharp aroma into the warm kitchen air.

Fifteen minutes later, when the pudding had cooled down and the nuts and raisins were added, Mr. Singh dished out three small bowls. Parm's mom and brother weren't home yet. "No need to tell them we tried a little before dinner," he said with a wink. "And anyway, it's so filling, you really can't eat more than a few bites at a time."

Gladys disagreed with this last statement—she was pretty sure she could have eaten the whole panful! Who knew carrots could taste so good? The halwa was like a warm, creamy version of carrot cake, except way better than any cake she'd ever tasted.

Mr. Singh invited Gladys for dinner, but sadly, she couldn't stay—when she called to say that she was going home with Parm, her mom had arranged to pick her up on the way home from work. So when Gladys heard the car horn honk outside, she thanked Mr. Singh for the container of halwa he had dished out for her. Parm followed her to the front door.

"What will you give Charissa the day after tomorrow?" Parm asked as Gladys pulled on her coat. "I don't think your parents will let you come over every night."

"They'll be out for a few hours at Parents' Night tomorrow," Gladys said. "So I should be able to throw something together while they're gone."

"Good luck," Parm said.

"Thanks," Gladys replied. "And thanks for getting your dad to teach me this recipe. It's amazing."

"I told you!" she cried. "No one can resist his gajar ka halwa!"

## Chapter 26

# THE SECRET NIGHTTIME PASTRY CHEF

CHARISSA SAVED A SPOT FOR GLADYS at lunch the next day and bypassed her salad to dig straight into the halwa. Gladys received several jealous glances (and a thumbs-up from Parm) when Charissa once again started an intense conversation with her about the dessert she was devouring.

"What is it? What's in it? How did you get it so creamy? What makes yellow raisins different from normal raisins?" Gladys could hardly keep up with the questions.

The next day would be Thursday, the day before Charissa made her decision, and Gladys intended to pull out all the stops. In her research on Classy Cakes,

★ ★ ★ ★

she had come across a collection of recipes by Allison Sconestein-Alforno, the bistro's head pastry chef. The recipe that caught Gladys's eye was called bluebarb crumble, made with blueberries and rhubarb.

Gladys knew that strawberry-rhubarb was a classic dessert combination, with the sweetness of the strawberries balancing the sourness of the rhubarb. But she'd never thought of using blueberries for sweetness instead, and the idea fascinated her. Plus, she thought it was a good idea to make one of the chef's recipes to get an idea of her style before reviewing her restaurant.

But it wasn't going to be easy. For starters, Gladys didn't have any of the right ingredients at home. And what's more, a crumble baking in the oven wafts its delicious smell all over the house, which is very nice—unless you're trying to keep your baking a secret, in which case it's very inconvenient.

At the end of the school day, Ms. Quincy made an announcement: "Now don't forget that tonight is Parents' Night for the sixth grade! Please remind your parents that we'll begin at six thirty p.m.—and that I won't tolerate tardiness from them any more than I do from you!"

The bell rang, and everyone stampeded for the doorway as usual. But as Gladys passed Ms. Quincy's desk, a wild idea struck her, and she slowed her steps until all of the other kids had left the room.

"Ms. Quincy?" she said. "I've been thinking about the letter you gave me."

The teacher looked up from her leopard-print briefcase. "Yes, Gladys?"

"Well," Gladys said, "you know how you wrote that teaching was your passion, even when you were a little girl? I was wondering . . . did your parents ever let you teach a class when you were a kid? In the one-room schoolhouse?"

Ms. Quincy smiled. "Why yes, they did, actually. Sometimes they'd even assign me a whole lesson to give the class, all on my own. My parents have always been my biggest supporters."

Gladys nodded. "That must be nice."

Ms. Quincy pushed her glasses farther up her nose and gave Gladys an appraising look. "Do your parents not support your dream, Gladys?" she asked. "Are they against the idea of your becoming a restaurant critic?"

"Oh, I don't think they even know about that," Gladys said quickly. "But they've never been happy about me spending time in the kitchen. And it's hard to, um . . . keep the flame of your passion alive, I guess, when you're not allowed to light a burner at home."

Ms. Quincy's smile returned. "That was a very nice metaphor."

"Oh," Gladys said, feeling her face grow warm. "Thank you."

"So," the teacher said shrewdly, "you'd like for me to speak to your parents about this issue tonight."

Gladys could hardly believe her luck—it had taken even less convincing than she'd thought. "Would you?" she asked. "Maybe you could ask them to stay after the Parents' Night meeting?"

"I can bring it up, Gladys," Ms. Quincy said, "but you must understand that your parents have the final say about how they run their house. You shouldn't count on my being able to convince them to change anything."

"I understand," Gladys said. Honestly, she didn't think that Ms. Quincy's opinion would make a bit of difference to her parents—but every extra minute she kept them out of the house was another minute Gladys could work on her crumble. "If you'll just talk to them as long as they'll listen, then maybe something will break through."

Ms. Quincy locked her briefcase and gave Gladys a sharp nod. "I'll do my best."

Unfortunately, rain had kept Gladys off her bike that morning, so she had to ride home with her mom and couldn't stop for groceries. She spent the next few hours finishing her homework so she'd be free to start on the crumble the moment her parents left for school.

Her parents, on the other hand, dawdled as long as they possibly could, and didn't leave the house until

6:22. "She hates tardiness!" Gladys cried, practically pushing them out the front door. Once their car was safely off the block, Gladys grabbed the cash her dad had left on the counter for pizza delivery and shot off on her bike through the darkening streets. She made it to Mr. Eng's just as he was locking the shop's front door.

"Gladys!" he cried. "What a pleasant surprise—two days in one week! How can I help you?"

"Crumblemergency!" Gladys blurted, gasping for breath. "Need rhubarb! And blueberries!"

Mr. Eng chuckled as he turned the key the other way, reopening the lock.

"It's not quite blueberry or rhubarb season yet here in the Northeast," he explained once they were inside the shop, "but I think I can help you." From the storeroom he produced some plump berries from Florida, and he dug a bag of frozen rhubarb pieces out of the freezer. Meanwhile, Gladys ran around the store grabbing sacks of flour and sugar, a stick of butter, and a handful of the black walnuts that she knew Charissa loved. The total came out to just about the amount she had in her pocket, and after handing her money over gratefully to Mr. Eng, she cycled home to get to work.

Thanks to birthday and Christmas gifts she had received from Aunt Lydia over the years, Gladys actually had some of the kitchen gear she needed for this project. She slid her stoneware baking pan out from the rack under the stove and retrieved her block of super-sharp Japanese knives from the crawl space. Picking one out to chop nuts with, she couldn't help remembering how horrified her mother had been when the set arrived on her ninth birthday. Her mom had immediately called Aunt Lydia to lecture her about how "inappropriate" it was to send "dangerous weapons" to a child, while her dad quickly stashed them away under the stairs. He said Gladys could have them back "when she was older"—but he never said *how much* older, so whenever Gladys snuck them out after that, she wasn't technically breaking the rules.

She was definitely breaking the rules when she turned the oven on, though. *Just this one time,* Gladys told herself. After all, it wasn't like she was cooking for pleasure—she had a job now.

The recipe wasn't particularly complicated, and less than an hour after she started, Gladys had a delicious-smelling crumble cooling out on the back patio. She wiped the kitchen down like it was a crime scene and ran around the house opening windows and turning on fans to let any lingering baking smells out. Finally, she brought the crumble back inside and scooped two large pieces. Following Mrs. Anderson's advice to always do a taste test, she ate one piece for dinner and put the other in a container for Charissa.

It only took one bite for Gladys to conclude that this crumble was the best thing she'd ever cooked. It was the perfect mix of sweet and sour, and even though Gladys didn't love walnuts, she had to admit they added just the right amount of crunch to the topping. But as she stashed the rest of it in the garage fridge, she wondered, *Will Charissa agree?*

Gladys's parents got home around nine thirty to find Gladys curled up on the sofa with her favorite book— the one about the large, sociable giant. "My goodness, that teacher of yours can *talk*!" her mom exclaimed as she kicked off her shoes and collapsed onto the recliner. "First it was the importance of education, then the importance of each subject specifically, then the strengths and weaknesses of each individual child . . . and she had the nerve to yell at Mr. Wall for falling asleep!"

Gladys grinned behind the pages of her book. That sounded like Ms. Quincy, all right.

"And then she wanted us to stay behind to talk even more," her dad complained, "but your mom had a craving for Sticky's, so we had to hurry to get there before it closed." He took off his glasses and rubbed his eyes. "How was your pizza, by the way?"

"Oh," Gladys said. She had her answer all prepared. "It was so good, I ate the whole thing."

Her mother's head whipped in her direction. "You did?"

"Uh-huh," Gladys lied, burying her nose deeper in her book so they wouldn't see her face. "And then I took the trash out. I figured you guys would be tired."

Her dad ruffled her hair. "That's our girl," he said. "The only kid on the block who voluntarily does extra chores!"

Gladys's mom didn't seem quite so tickled by her response—but she also looked way too exhausted to go outside and check the trash for a pizza box. She shrugged a padded shoulder. "We are tired, it's true," she said. "Thanks, honey." Then she pushed herself up, shuffled past the kitchen without checking for signs of cooking, and climbed the stairs to bed. A moment later, Gladys's dad followed.

Gladys let out an enormous sigh of relief. She'd been lucky—this time.

Gladys was nervous to present the crumble to Charissa the next day. Maybe she should have gone with a less unusual flavor, like cherry or apple. Charissa had a sophisticated palate, but was bluebarb asking her to stretch her taste buds too far?

As Charissa chewed her first bite, her face went through many expressions. She puckered up at the tang of the rhubarb, but then smiled at the sweetness of the berries; her eyes lit up at a hint of cinnamon, then closed dreamily as the nutty topping crunched between her teeth.

Gladys couldn't help herself. "Do you like it?" she burst out after what felt like an hour of silence. Charissa's head turned slowly just as Gladys remembered what happened to the last girl who interrupted Charissa's dessert.

But Charissa had no harsh words for Gladys—she had no words at all. Instead, she threw her arms around her and squeezed for a long minute.

"Thank you," Charissa finally whispered in Gladys's ear, and Gladys realized that was probably the first time she had ever heard Charissa thank anyone for anything.

"Um, no problem," Gladys murmured. "I'm really glad you like it."

She *was* glad, and not just because it increased her chances of getting to New York City and Classy Cakes. In fact, "the plan" had totally slipped Gladys's mind for the moment, and she simply basked in the feeling of having her cooking appreciated by another person. When she had cooked all those other meals in the past, Gladys only had herself to feed and give feedback on how a recipe turned out. But Charissa not only devoured Gladys's cooking, she even seemed interested in learning how it was made.

"So what's it called?" Charissa started.

"Bluebarb crumble."

"Bluebarb?"

"It's short for blueberry-rhubarb."

"What's rhubarb?"

"Well," Gladys began, "it looks kind of like celery, but you can't eat it raw. It tastes sour, and it grows like a weed . . ."

Their discussion lasted for the rest of the lunch period. When the bell rang, Charissa said, almost meekly, "Gladys? Um, do you think that instead of something new, I could have some more of this blue-barb stuff tomorrow?"

"Of course!" Gladys cried, thinking about all the left-over crumble in the garage. She wouldn't mind having a night off from the stresses of secret dessert-making.

At recess the next day, her belly full of another serving of bluebarb crumble, Charissa climbed back up onto her mound of pebbles and turned to address the crowd.

Gladys stood near the back of the group next to Parm, who insisted she was "just along to watch the circus." As she waited for the announcement, Gladys caught snatches of whispered conversations around her.

"Who d'you think it'll be?" one voice said.

"I dunno," said a second, "but have you noticed that Charissa's been, like, less horrible this week than usual?"

"Yeah!" a third voice hissed. "I mean, I wouldn't say she's been nice or anything, but she hasn't made fun of anyone . . ."

"Yeah, or told anyone to shut up . . ."

". . . in almost three days! I wonder what's gotten into her?"

*Crumble,* Gladys thought happily. *And halwa, and pancakes . . .*

Charissa cleared her throat, and all the whispering died. "I've made my decision," she said simply, and her eyes scanned the crowd until they found the person they were looking for. "Gladys, you're in."

Charissa jumped off the mound, and the crowd parted before her, fallen faces and tear-filled eyes watching as she made a beeline for Gladys.

"The limo will pick you up tomorrow at six," Charissa said, crisp and businesslike. "Wear purple."

Gladys's voice didn't seem to be working, so she simply nodded. But this must have been an acceptable response because Charissa said, "Good." Then, after flashing Gladys a grin so brief that Gladys later thought she might have imagined it, Charissa took off across the playground, alone.

The eyes of most of the sixth-grade girls (and quite a few boys who had also turned up for the big announcement) were now on Gladys Gatsby, a person most of them forgot existed most of the time. And suddenly those eyes were looking a lot less teary and a lot more . . . thirsty. Not thirsty for a milk shake, or a juice box. Thirsty for blood.

"Come on," Parm whispered, grabbing Gladys's arm and dragging her away from the crowd. "This mob looks like it might attack."

Feeling triumphant and embarrassed, thrilled and confused all at the same time, Gladys let Parm pull her away to the relative safety of the space beneath the monkey bars.

## Chapter 27

# PLAN A IS TOAST

GLADYS WAS WAITING BY THE WINDOW when the limo pulled up to her house the next day at precisely six p.m. She had seen limos on TV and in movies and was expecting it to be black or white, but to her surprise it was eggplant purple with green trim, as if Barney the Dinosaur had swallowed a stretched-out Cadillac.

"They're here!" Gladys called. She knew her parents wanted to thank the Bentleys for including Gladys in the birthday outing.

Gladys's mom had been visibly shocked when Gladys told them that she was invited to a Broadway show for Charissa Bentley's birthday, simply because Gladys hardly ever got invited to anyone's

★ ★ ★ ★

birthday party. Gladys's dad, on the other hand, was more shocked that anyone would spend that much money on a party for a twelve-year-old.

"Oh, hush, George," Gladys's mom said. "I just think it's wonderful that Gladys is making new friends!"

"New friends who are apparently millionaires," her husband grumbled. "Gladdy, you'd better not expect a party like that for your twelfth."

"Don't worry, Dad," Gladys said. "Like I've said, all I want for my birthday is permission to bake my own birthday cake." Gladys's birthday wasn't until June— after her kitchen ban was set to expire—but she figured that it couldn't hurt to start lobbying for this privilege early.

While Gladys was putting on her peacoat, the limousine sounded its horn, which played "Happy Birthday to You" loudly for the whole neighborhood to hear. Gladys grabbed her purse (which held her all-important journal and pencil) and Charissa's present. Then the whole family trooped out to the front lawn just as the Bentleys emerged from the limo door.

Mr. Bentley came out first. A portly man with a bald head, he was dressed in a dark suit and overcoat and a bright purple tie that matched the limousine.

Mrs. Bentley emerged next, in a full-length velvet ball gown and matching wrap in a rich shade of plum.

She was a tall woman with glossy auburn hair swept into an elegant updo.

Charissa came out last. She wore a poufy purple dress, her soft purple coat, and sparkling purple Mary Janes, and her regular high ponytail was done in bouncy ringlet curls. Her lips shimmered with gloss, and pale purple shadow colored her eyelids.

Mr. Bentley shook hands with Gladys's dad. "Mr. Gatsby," he said gruffly.

"Mr. Bentley," Gladys's dad replied. "Er, nice ride."

"This ridiculous thing? Ha!" Mr. Bentley jerked his thumb back toward the limo. "Do you have any idea how much it costs to rent per hour?"

"Why, the question never crossed my mind," Gladys's dad said.

Gladys's mom was talking to Mrs. Bentley. "Thank you so much for inviting Gladys tonight. I know that she's *so* excited to be included!"

Mrs. Bentley shrugged one velvet-wrapped shoulder. "I was surprised that Charissa didn't pick one of her other friends. But I guess she wanted your daughter to come, and whatever Charissa wants, Charissa gets!"

And Gladys was talking to Charissa. "Happy birthday," she said, handing Charissa a wrapped package. Inside was a sequined purple purse that Gladys's mother had picked out that morning at the department store where she'd also bought Gladys her own purple dress for the outing. As much as Gladys didn't like Charissa telling her what to wear, in this case she figured it was a small price to pay for a ride to New York City. And at least the dress wasn't terribly poufy.

Charissa tore into the present immediately. "Cool," she said when she pulled out the purse. "It matches my shoes." Then she tossed her curly ponytail and looked at Gladys expectantly.

Gladys wasn't sure what else to say or do. She hadn't really prepared for the part of the night when she'd have to talk to Charissa and her family. Instead, she'd spent every spare moment that day with Sandy, formulating her plan for getting to Classy Cakes once she made it to New York City.

The plan was this: Shortly after the Broadway show started, Gladys would tell the Bentleys that she needed to use the bathroom; then she would slip outside and run to Classy Cakes (which, luckily, was only three blocks from the theater). There would be no time to sit down and eat, so instead Gladys would head straight to the takeout counter and order one of everything on the menu. While her order was being filled, she would observe everything about the restaurant's décor and service that she possibly could. Then, once she had her desserts in a bag, she would ask to use the restaurant's bathroom. Hidden in a stall, she would take one bite of every dessert and write down her impressions as best she could. Finally, she would dispose of the evidence in a trash can and run back to the theater just in time for the play's intermission, when she would find the Bentleys and tell them that she felt *so* much better now, thank you.

They had been over the plan about a hundred times, and Sandy and Gladys agreed that it was the best they could do. Still, it was far from perfect. Wolfing mouthfuls from takeout containers while locked in a toilet stall didn't really sound like the best way to taste delicate desserts.

"Don't worry about that!" Sandy had exclaimed. "If the food's good, it'll be good wherever you eat it. Worry about getting your butt back in your seat at the theater before the Bentleys call the cops on you!"

Of course, the plan had no chance of working if Gladys didn't make it into the city—and, she realized as she stood under the weight of Charissa's stare, it wasn't too late for Charissa to change her mind. They were still in East Dumpsford . . . one word from Charissa and the limo could pull away from the Gatsbys' house and swing across town to pick up Rolanda, or Marti, or anyone else of Charissa's choosing.

Gladys gulped. *Say something!* her brain screamed. *Anything!*

"Edamame!" she cried.

"What?" Charissa asked.

"Oh, nothing, sorry." Apparently, her subconscious

was filled with steamed soybeans. "Can I see the inside of the limo?"

At this, Charissa brightened. "Sure!" she said. "It's awesome. It's purple on the inside, too! Daddy had to call around to rental companies in three different states to find one like this."

The inside of the limo was indeed very purple, and very plush. There was an icebox with sodas and fancy chilled glasses, and a TV that came down from the ceiling. There was enough room for everyone to lie down if they wanted to, and when Charissa pressed a button on the ceiling, a sunroof yawned open. The girls kicked off their shoes and climbed up on the seats to stick their heads out into the night air.

Outside, the adults were now standing in a little circle. "So, what show are you taking the girls to?" Gladys's mom asked.

"It's called *Glossy Girl: The Musical,*" Mrs. Bentley answered. "It's the first musical ever to be based on a teen magazine."

"Is that so?" said Gladys's dad.

"Oh, yes," replied Mrs. Bentley excitedly. "There have been musicals based on books and movies, but never on a teen magazine. The *Dumpsford Township Intelligencer* called it 'a pioneering triumph!'"

"And the *New York Standard* called it 'the worst musical in the history of Broadway,'" grumbled Mr. Bentley, who seemed much less excited.

"We don't read the *New York Standard,*" said Gladys's dad.

"We don't, either," said Mr. Bentley, "but my cousin, Bradford Bentley, happens to be the theater critic there. This show's been sold out for months, and he was the only one who could get us tickets. He showed me his review to try to convince us to see something else, but Charissa only wanted *Glossy Girl,* and what Charissa wants . . ." He sighed. "Charissa gets."

"We should get going, dear," Mrs. Bentley said, and after another round of handshakes, they climbed back into the limo.

The girls waved good-bye to Gladys's parents through the sunroof as the car pulled away, then settled back down into the purple cushions. Minutes later, the limo merged onto the expressway. *It's really happening,* Gladys thought. She was on her way to New York City to visit the first real restaurant of her reviewing career.

By the time the limo got close to the tunnel that would take them into Manhattan, it had slowed to a crawl. Mr. Bentley muttered about the traffic, and Mrs. Bentley reassured him that they had factored in plenty of extra time to get to the theater. "Time that I'm paying for," Mr. Bentley grumbled.

Charissa didn't hear, or at least pretended not to hear, her father's complaints. She was too busy raiding the icebox for soda, flipping through the TV channels, and generally talking Gladys's ear off about how excited she was to finally be twelve.

"I'm gonna be a counselor-in-training at Camp Bentley this year, which means I get a whole new uniform . . . no more barrettes, barrettes are for babies, from now on it's headbands all the way . . . ankle socks are out, knee socks are in . . . really, anyone who's *serious* about being twelve should get a whole new wardrobe! I read that in *Glossy Girl.* Gladys, are you listening?"

"Yes!" cried Gladys, who had of course been reviewing her plan and only been half listening at best. Luckily, she'd caught the last thing Charissa said. "Whole new wardrobe, got it!"

"Good," Charissa said. And then, "Hey, look! It's the show we're going to see!" Gladys looked to the TV screen to see an army of teenagers wearing headbands and knee socks jumping around a stage and singing a very annoying song.

*"Dancin' to the beat of a teenage heart—yeah!"* Charissa sang along. "I have the sound track, and I know all the songs by heart. Hey, Mommy, let's listen to it now!"

"Great idea!" cried Mrs. Bentley, who had been tapping one high-heeled foot along to the commercial. She fished her phone out of her purse and plugged it into the limo's audio jack. A minute later, Charissa was singing along to the opening number ("U Can't Tame a Glossy Girl!"), and Mr. Bentley was massaging his temples. Gladys listened as patiently as she could—she figured it was the least she could do, considering she was planning to miss a big chunk of the live show.

The limo finally pulled up to the theater at seven forty-five. Mrs. Bentley shepherded her husband and the girls into the lobby, where they had to fight through a crowd to get to the ticket-taker.

Once they were finally inside the main auditorium, things were a little calmer—an usher handed them programs and showed them to their seats. "Here we are!" he cried cheerfully, waving the Bentleys and Gladys into the third row. The seats were, as Charissa had claimed at school, excellent—close to the stage and in the exact center of the theater. However, that also meant they were nowhere near an aisle. Gladys did a quick count and realized she would have to climb over a lot of legs to get out from her seat sandwiched in between Charissa and Mrs. Bentley. *Fudge,* Gladys thought. In her planning with Sandy, she'd imagined herself sitting much closer to an aisle.

According to the program, there was a fifteen-minute intermission one hour into the show. Gladys and Sandy had estimated that, if she was fast, Gladys might be able to get to Classy Cakes, do her tasting, and get back to the theater in thirty minutes, but that it would probably take more like forty-five. That meant she had to escape within the first thirty minutes of the show to have any hope of getting back to her seat by the end of intermission.

All of the seats around Gladys and the Bentleys were filling up fast. The crowd was mostly made up of kids around Gladys's age, their slightly apprehensive-looking parents, and several sets of terrified-looking grandparents. "Have you seen this song list?" Gladys heard the white-haired man in front of her ask the silver-haired lady next to him. "'Make-Up for Making Out'? 'Ten Tips for the Perfect Party'? What are we doing here?"

"Just remember to turn off your hearing aid the *moment* the music starts," the lady said. "That's what Mabel did last week when she came with her granddaughter, and she made it through just fine."

Then the lights dimmed and the orchestra started up with the opening drumbeats of "U Can't Tame a Glossy Girl!"

"Turn it off now, *now!*" the old lady hissed as she and the man fumbled for their ears.

The musical was filled with bright lights, loud music, and songs that didn't make any sense, since they were based on magazine articles instead of a story with a plot. The cartwheeling actors and actresses who made up the cast were supposed to be playing teenagers, but from the third row you could see through the layers of makeup that most of them were way older than that. (One "teen," according to his bio in the program, had just finished performing in *The Phantom of the Opera* for twelve years straight. Still, he cartwheeled and screeched with the best of them.)

The kids in the audience clapped and sang along while parents glanced at watches and grandparents dozed. Gladys checked her watch, too, as often as she dared, the butterflies in her stomach growing more and more fluttery with every passing minute.

Finally, at 8:26, she couldn't wait any longer: it was time to make her move. She was five seats off the aisle on Mrs. Bentley's side and eight seats off on Charissa's side; so, as soon as there was a brief lull between songs, she leaned toward Mrs. Bentley and half stood up. "Excuse me," she said quietly, "I need to go to the bathroom."

But Mrs. Bentley didn't budge. "Not now," she said simply. "It's the middle of the show."

Gladys was flustered—this wasn't the response she'd expected! "But, um, I really need to go . . ." she stammered. Then, trying to sound more forceful, she added, "Now!"

"Just try to hold it," Mrs. Bentley said coolly. "It's almost intermission."

"Actually," Gladys hissed back, "intermission's not for another thirty-four min—" but her words were drowned out by a crash of cymbals. The orchestra started blasting a new song, and someone tapped Gladys sharply on the shoulder and whispered for her to sit down.

She couldn't believe it. Mrs. Bentley really wasn't going to let her out! As she sank helplessly back into her seat, she mentally cursed the person who designed the theater with rows so narrow that you couldn't get out without the cooperation of the person next to you, unless you wanted to crawl over her lap or under her legs. Gladys considered both of these options, but quickly dismissed them. They'd cause too much of a scene, and she wanted to slip away as quietly as possible so that hopefully the Bentleys would forget she was even gone.

Gladys only had one choice left: She'd have to try to get out on Charissa's side. The new song seemed to go on forever, but when it finally ended (*8:34!* Gladys's watch screamed), Gladys leaned over to the right. "Sorry, Charissa," she whispered, "I need to go to the bathroom. Can I squeeze out?"

Charissa turned to look at her with wide eyes. "But you can't go *now*!" she insisted. "You'll miss 'Rock the Teenage World,' and that's the best number in the whole show! Oh, look, it's starting!" And she grabbed Gladys's arm excitedly as a woman in a fluorescent orange tank top backflipped across the stage to a blaring electric guitar.

Charissa's grip was strong. Gladys wasn't going anywhere.

"Rock the Teenage World" was an epic number, complete with indoor fireworks and dancing in the aisles. Charissa squealed with delight and gripped Gladys harder with each new flash or bang. Gladys could only jealously watch the dancers, moving so freely up and down the aisles, as time ticked away.

8:40 . . . 8:50 . . .

Gladys's stomach now seemed to lurch in time with the dancers' high kicks. *Okay,* she thought to herself. *Plan A is toast. Burnt, charred, blackened toast. Time for Plan B.*

Clearly, she couldn't get out until intermission; she'd just have to make her escape then and visit Classy Cakes during the second half of the show. The second half was shorter—only forty-five minutes, according to the program—but if all went well, she should be able to get back with a little time to spare.

When the curtain came down and the lights came up at 9 p.m., Gladys was ready to sprint. She had her purse—containing her journal and her life savings in cash—over her shoulder and waited impatiently while the audience finished applauding. But then the aisles got jammed within seconds. Kids, wanting snacks and souvenir T-shirts, pulled their parents this way and that, and everyone tripped over the sleepy grandparents who were slowly making their way to the bathrooms. It took Gladys's row almost five minutes to clear.

"Okay, I'm going to the bathroom," Gladys said to the Bentleys when they finally reached the aisle. She turned to go when, to her horror, she heard Charissa say, "Hang on, I have to go, too!"

"So do I," Mrs. Bentley announced. "We'll all go together." And just like that, Mrs. Bentley's hand was gripping Gladys's shoulder, guiding her to the back of the theater.

Gladys went along miserably, her eyes darting around for possible escape routes. The bathrooms were on the lower level, and the stairs were extremely crowded—it took them another three minutes just to get down. Mrs. Bentley was grasping both girls at this point to keep from being separated, and she didn't let go.

The line for the women's room snaked out the door and halfway across the lounge. Mrs. Bentley groaned when she saw it, but there was nothing they could do. It inched forward at a slow but steady pace, and finally, after another few minutes, they were inside.

The bathroom only had three stalls, and as the door to the middle one opened, they heard a set of chimes over the theater's sound system. "We'll have to be fast," Mrs. Bentley said. "That sound means the show is about to start again." Charissa, who looked horrified at the idea of missing even a minute of the second half, let out a yelp and dove into the free stall. The door on the right opened next, and Mrs. Bentley practically shoved Gladys in the moment its occupant emerged.

Gladys stood in the stall and tried to think. She heard a toilet flush on the other end of the bathroom and a door squeak open, then the clack of Mrs. Bentley's heels as she took over that stall. A second set of chimes sounded.

Gladys had hoped to spend some time in a bathroom stall that night, just not this one. If only she could teleport herself from one locked bathroom stall to another one three blocks away! But Gladys knew that she needed to pull herself together and come up with yet another plan. If she let the Bentleys drag her back upstairs, she would never get to Classy Cakes.

She looked around wildly for inspiration. She was in the corner stall. Behind the toilet, over her head, was a small window, propped open to lend a breath of air to the stuffy bathroom.

A series of flushes and squeaks told Gladys that Charissa and her mother had both emerged from their stalls into the now-empty bathroom. She heard the sink water running briefly and then the rumble of a paper towel being pulled from its dispenser.

"Gladys?" Mrs. Bentley called. "Time to go!"

Gladys took a deep breath. It was now or never. "I need a few more minutes," she called back. "I'm not feeling so great. But you guys go back without me! I don't want you to miss the show!"

"Nonsense," Mrs. Bentley replied firmly. "If you're sick, we'll stay with you. What exactly is the matter?"

"It's . . . it's nothing, really," Gladys called. "My stomach hurts a little. I'll be fine, you should go!"

The chimes sounded for a third time, and Gladys heard Charissa whimper, "Mom-*my* . . ."

Mrs. Bentley sighed. Was she changing her mind? Gladys decided to make one last plea. "Please, don't let me ruin Charissa's birthday!" she called through the stall door. "I'll see you upstairs as soon as I feel better!"

There was a moment of silence, and then Mrs. Bentley said, "All right. Come on, Charissa, let's scoot!" Heels clacked, and a flood of relief washed over Gladys as the bathroom door opened and shut. Finally, she was alone.

She supposed she could wait until they got back to their seats, then dash upstairs and out the front door—but with all this time already wasted, every second mattered. In a moment, she was up on the toilet seat, then pushing the little window all the way open. Finally, slinging her purse over one shoulder, Gladys hoisted herself up over the sill and tumbled into the middle of New York City.

# Chapter 28

## CLASSY CAKES

GLADYS LANDED ON HER HANDS AND knees and jumped up to brush herself off. A quick look around told her that she was in an alleyway next to the theater. To her left was a large Dumpster, and to her right was the theater's stage door— beside which two actors and an actress, coats thrown on over their neon tank tops, stood sipping from bottles of water and staring at her.

"Sneaking out at halftime, eh?" said the taller actor, raising an eyebrow.

"Well," the actress said, "she isn't the first!"

All three laughed, shaking their heads. Standing just a few feet away, they looked even older than they had onstage.

★ ★ ★ ★

"Brooke would sneak out if she could," said the shorter actor, elbowing the actress.

"So would you," said Brooke.

The taller actor sighed. "I can't believe I left *Phantom* for this."

"Oh, don't start with that again, Mike," Brooke groaned. Then she turned to Gladys. "Look, it's not our fault the show sucks, okay? We didn't write it."

"Nobody wrote it!" shrieked the shorter actor. "That's the problem!"

Gladys felt sorry for the miserable actors but couldn't stand there all night listening to them complain—she had her own writing to do, and needed to figure out where she was going. "Excuse me," she said, "but which way is Ninth Avenue?"

The shorter actor jerked his thumb over his shoulder, then pointed to the left.

"Thanks!" Gladys cried, and hurried past the group. She was almost at the end of the alley when she paused—something about this situation didn't make sense.

"Sorry," she said, turning back to them, "but if you really hate being in the show, why do you all look so happy onstage?"

"Kid," said Brooke, tossing her bottle into the Dumpster, "that's why they call it *acting*."

The streets were blazingly lit with streetlights, and the sidewalks were full of people. Gladys darted around people in long coats and short coats, puffy coats and sleek coats. Her peacoat was in her seat at the theater, but she didn't feel cold—she didn't feel much of anything but her heart racing and her legs pumping. At Ninth Avenue, she turned left to run the final block. Near the corner she could see a large crowd of people jostling underneath a yellow-and-black polka-dotted awning. When she got closer, she saw the words CLASSY CAKES written across the awning in elegant script.

She'd made it! She was there! Unfortunately, so were about a hundred other people. At the door to the restaurant, a young woman in a yellow blouse and black skirt was trying to make an announcement. "Excuse me! Hello!" she was calling. Finally, the crowd quieted enough to hear her.

"There is currently a three-hour wait for tables if you do not have a reservation!" she shouted. Some people in the crowd groaned, and a few walked away. But most stayed. The woman was still yelling, something about putting your name on a list. Suddenly, the crowd surged forward, pinning her against the glass door. "One at a time, one at a time!" she shrieked as people pushed and shoved to get their names on the list.

Using her small size to her advantage, Gladys elbowed her way into the mob and squeezed over, under, and through until she was standing in front of the woman with the clipboard. A small name tag on the woman's blouse said MOIRA.

"Excuse me," Gladys said as politely as she could. But Moira, busy scribbling names, clearly didn't hear her. So Gladys was forced to shout.

"EXCUSE ME!"

Moira looked up briefly. "Three-hour wait," she said, then turned back to her clipboard.

"Sorry!" Gladys shouted with a smile. "But I don't need a table! I'm just here to get takeout!"

"We don't do takeout," Moira snapped, not even looking up from her board this time.

Gladys felt dizzy. Every restaurant she knew in East Dumpsford offered takeout; it had never occurred to her that a restaurant in New York City might not.

"But," Gladys started again, "I really need—"

In one quick movement, Moira lowered her clipboard and looked Gladys straight in the face. "Little girl, let me make it real simple for you. Do you have a reservation?"

"No, but—"

"Then it's a Three. Hour. Wait."

With that, Moira straightened back up and smoothed her skirt. "Thanks for your patience!" she shouted at the crowd. "We'll see some of you in three hours!" And she yanked the door open and disappeared into the restaurant.

The crowd began to disperse, carrying Gladys a short way down the street with it. She looked through one of the restaurant's plate glass windows. At the table just inside, a young couple shared each other's desserts: she fed him a bite from a tall slice of cake, then he scooped her a spoonful of his parfait. The woman closed her eyes with an expression of perfect contentment and licked her lips.

This happy scene made Gladys snap. She had not worked so hard to get the spot in Charissa's limo and gone through so much trouble to sneak out of the theater just to watch other people eat dessert! She wasn't going to let Moira and the three-hour wait stop her; she wasn't giving up yet.

Gladys marched back to the restaurant's front door and let herself in. Moira, who was now standing behind a small podium, looked up when she felt the draft and said irritably, "There's a THREE-HOUR— Oh, it's you again."

Gladys took a moment to observe her surroundings. To Moira's left was the dining room filled with people, a comfortable-looking area with wrought iron tables and chairs and subtly polka-dotted tablecloths and napkins. To her right were double doors that, based on the clanging noises coming from behind them, Gladys thought must lead to the kitchen.

"Can I help you with something?" Moira asked in a tone that made it clear she didn't want to help Gladys at all.

"Yes," Gladys answered. "I'd like to use the restroom, please."

"Sorry," Moira said. "Restrooms are for customers only."

"But I *am* a customer!" Gladys said. "I forgot, but I do have a reservation. I mean, my parents do. They're at the theater now, but they're going to come meet me here after." Gladys was pretty pleased with this story, which she'd just come up with on the spot.

Moira's eyes narrowed. "What are their names?" she asked.

"Who?"

"Your parents. The people who made the reservation."

"Oh. Um . . . Bentley!" Gladys blurted, saying the first name she could think of that wasn't her own. "Our last name is Bentley."

"Bentley, huh?" said Moira, smirking. "Well, let me just see if I can find you . . ." And she turned a page in the large book on the podium labeled RESERVATIONS.

"Look," Gladys stammered, "they're kind of absent-minded. I *think* they made a reservation. I mean, I know that they *meant* to make a—" But she was cut off as a man dressed in white burst out of the kitchen door.

"Moira!" he said breathlessly. "Allison needs to

see you out back ASAP. Something about the—"
Suddenly he noticed Gladys standing there and lowered his voice to a whisper. "Something about the C-O-O-K-I-E-S."

Gladys couldn't help herself. "You know, I *can* spell," she said. The man ignored her.

Moira slammed the reservations book shut. "You wait here," she commanded Gladys, and followed the man back to the kitchen.

Of course, Gladys didn't wait there—and she didn't go to the restroom, either. She headed straight into the dining room.

The room was lit mostly by candles and swirly-looking light fixtures along the walls, and it took her eyes a moment to adjust to the dimness. But when they did, she saw that the couple at the window was leaving their table. The man took the woman's hand, and Gladys jumped to one side to let them pass. The woman had left a large bite of cake on her plate.

Gladys glanced around. The place was packed, and waiters and waitresses were hurrying about, but no one seemed to be paying any attention to her. So she strolled casually over to the now-empty table, reached out her hand—no time for forks!—and shoved the bite of cake into her mouth.

Tastes of allspice, pistachio, and cardamom—yes, definitely cardamom—burst onto her tongue, and the cake's moist, almost juicy texture helped it go down easily. Then Gladys noticed there was a dollop of parfait left in the glass across the table. Did she dare? She looked around again and, when she saw no one watching, helped herself to a spoonful of the velvety, raspberry-flavored dessert.

Across the room, an older couple was rising, the man helping the woman with her coat. From what Gladys could see, they were leaving even more dessert behind than the young couple! As soon as they were a few steps away from their table, Gladys swooped in. She hurriedly gobbled up several bites of a lavender-scented, lemon-flavored custard, then moved on to the chunk of a nutty tart that was sitting on the other plate. Who were these people who left half of their delicious (and expensive) desserts on their plates?

But there was no time to wonder—a party of four was leaving in the middle of the room. Gladys could see a dish half-full of melting ice cream, several cookies, a mini fruit tart, and the remains of a cheese plate. *Jackpot,* she thought, and had taken two steps in that direction when she spotted Moira leading a pair of women to their seats at the now-cleared table by the window.

*Fudge!*

In a flash, Gladys backtracked and ducked underneath the last table. The polka-dotted tablecloth reached halfway to the floor, so it didn't hide her completely, but Gladys hoped that, in the low lighting, it would be enough to keep her out of sight until Moira was gone.

Gladys stayed there for a minute, watching the black-clad legs of the serving staff hurry back and forth. Then, just when she felt reasonably sure that it was safe to come out, a pair of those legs stopped right beside her. The dishes above her head clattered as the legs' owner cleared them away. When the legs finally left, she prepared to crawl out again, but almost instantly three new pairs of legs were blocking her exit.

"Please, have a seat," Gladys heard Moira coo. "And I hope you enjoy your dessert!"

The chairs next to Gladys scraped back, and a moment later the space under the table was a lot more crowded. It was the woman's feet, clad in pointy-toed, zebra-striped pumps, that kicked Gladys first.

"Is that you, Bernard?" the woman asked.

"Is what me?" said Bernard.

"Is that you that I'm kicking?" And she kicked again, this time catching Gladys in the shoulder. Gladys stifled a groan.

"Um, no," Bernard answered.

"Well, what the heck is it, then?" And the woman reared up for a third kick. But Gladys was ready this time—she grabbed the woman's shoe as it came toward her face and yanked it right off.

The woman screamed. In seconds, more feet came running toward the table. "My shoe!" the woman screeched. "There's something down there, and it's eaten my shoe!"

It was Moira who lifted the tablecloth. "You!" she cried. "Come out of there right now! And leave that shoe!"

Gladys knew that the game was up, and she did as she was told. Moira grabbed Gladys by one arm, and a busboy took her by the other. "Out!" Moira cried. "Out, out, out!" Half escorting, half carrying, they brought Gladys to the nearest emergency exit and shoved her into the cold.

The one-way door slammed shut and, for the second time that night, Gladys found herself in an alleyway, standing next to a Dumpster.

Her breath puffed visibly in front of her as she sighed. On the one hand, she was proud of herself for having gotten into the restaurant—proud that even with Mrs. Bentley and Moira trying to stop her, she had managed to get her taste buds on a few of Classy Cakes's unique desserts. But she also knew that she didn't have enough material to write a review. Classy Cakes had more than twenty desserts on its menu, and Gladys had only tasted four. If only she'd had the chance to try a few more! But she hadn't, and there was no way she'd be able to come back before her deadline.

She had failed, and would have to e-mail Fiona Inglethorpe and admit it.

The editor would find another critic to review Classy Cakes—someone who lived in New York City, who could visit without any sneaking; someone who made reservations; someone who wasn't a sixth-grader at East Dumpsford Elementary.

Gladys checked her watch: 9:33. If she hurried, she could get back for the show's finale and find the Bentleys before they called the police and reported her missing. She jogged to the end of the alley, turned right, and took off for the theater.

Ten minutes later, Gladys was standing in the lobby. The ticket-taker was nowhere in sight, so she quietly let herself into the darkened theater. She was about to slip down the aisle when she felt a strong hand on her shoulder and looked around to see an usher's uniform.

"What do you think you're doing?" the usher hissed. "The finale's about to start—you wanna get trampled?"

"Trampled?" Gladys asked, but no sooner had she spoken than the house lights burst on and more indoor fireworks exploded with a deafening roar. "Teenagers" poured into the aisles from every direction. Some leapt off the stage while others tore in from the back and sides of the theater. The usher grabbed Gladys and flattened her against the wall next to him as one actor after another cartwheeled past.

"Thanks!" Gladys shouted.

"No problem!" the usher shouted back. "We don't want any more fatalities!"

Gladys recognized the last person to burst in from the back—it was the shorter actor from the stage door. "Hey!" he cried as he danced past Gladys. "You came back!" He looked pleased . . . but maybe that was just more acting.

Gladys stayed with the usher until the last fire-cracker sounded and the show, thankfully, was over. Then, tired of fighting crowds, she stayed where she was and let the Bentleys come to her.

Charissa was the first one to spot her. "Gladys!" she cried, running over. "Where have you been?"

"Yes, Gladys, where *have* you been?" Mrs. Bentley asked sharply.

Gladys had her answer ready. "I tried to get back, but the usher wouldn't let me—with all the dancing in the aisles, he said it was too dangerous."

"Ah," said Mrs. Bentley. "Well, I guess that makes sense."

"Come on, Gladys, let's go," Charissa said. She also seemed to find Gladys's explanation believable. "Did you see the part when the teenagers did a photo shoot at the beach? How awesome was that? And then there was the part . . ." By the time Charissa finished telling Gladys about all her favorite parts, Gladys felt like she hadn't missed any of the show at all.

The purple limo was waiting for them half a block

away. People were crowded around it, trying to get a look through the tinted windows to see if there was a celebrity inside.

"Out of our way, out of our way!" Mr. Bentley shouted. Before the driver could rush around and open the door for him, he yanked it open himself and shoved them inside.

They pulled away from the curb with a jerk and started down the street. "The driver knows where to go, right, Daddy?" Charissa asked.

"Yes, cupcake, I gave him the address," Mr. Bentley said.

"Where *are* we going?" Gladys asked. She hadn't thought much about the night beyond the Broadway show.

Charissa laughed. "We're going wherever I *say* we go!"

The limo turned left, then right, then stopped abruptly. "What's the matter?" Gladys asked.

"Nothing's the matter!" Charissa said brightly. "We're here!"

They all piled back out of the car—first Mrs. Bentley, then Mr. Bentley, then Charissa, and finally Gladys. As she stepped out, the first thing she saw was a yellow awning with black polka dots.

She gazed up in awe as Charissa chattered nonstop into her ear. "So I searched for 'bluebarb crumble' online and found out that the chef who invented it has her own restaurant! I told Daddy that he *had* to get us a reservation, and even Mommy said it would be okay to break the salad diet on my birthday. It's called Classy Cakes, and the *whole* menu is desserts! How awesome is that?"

Gladys threw her arms around Charissa.

"Charissa," she said, "that is the *most* awesome thing I have ever heard."

# Chapter 29

# EVERYTHING ON THE MENU

LATER THAT NIGHT, AS THE LIMOUSINE glided back toward East Dumpsford, Gladys made a mental list of all her favorite moments from her second visit to Classy Cakes.

There was the moment when Moira's jaw dropped as they all walked into the restaurant, and Charissa's father said, "Bentley, party of four—we have a reservation."

There was the moment when the waiter came to their table and said, "Well, folks, what can I get you this evening?" and Charissa said, "We'll have one of everything on the menu."

"Um," the waiter stammered, looking over at Mr. and Mrs. Bentley.

★ ★ ★ ★

"It's her birthday!" Mrs. Bentley said, beaming.

Mr. Bentley nodded. "And whatever Charissa wants, Charissa gets."

Gladys had to restrain herself from leaping across the table and hugging them, too.

And there was the moment when the desserts began to arrive, carried by a procession of servers in black and yellow. Creamy-looking custards were followed by beautifully decorated slices of cake. Crisp-shelled pastries were set down next to gooey-centered pies. Dainty little goblets featuring ice cream and sorbet came out on a silver tray, and a pungent aroma rose off a long wooden board that was dotted with more kinds of cheese than Gladys had ever seen, even in Mr. Eng's special fridge.

Over the next two hours, Gladys and the Bentleys ate their way through the entire menu. True to her original plan, Gladys tried at least one bite of every dessert. She ended up slipping off to the bathroom three times to write down more extensive notes—there were so many details she didn't want to forget!—but luckily, since she had already been "sick" earlier in the evening, no one questioned her about these trips.

Everyone at the table had a different favorite in the end: Charissa loved the tree-nut tart, Mr. Bentley devoured the ginger-sultana bread pudding, and Mrs. Bentley favored the papaya–passion fruit sorbet.

Gladys noted them all down in her journal, along with her own favorite, which she planned to mention specially in her review.

The limo pulled into her driveway at three a.m., and Gladys dug her house key out of her purse. A light was still shining in the hallway, and to her surprise, she found both of her parents asleep on the living room sofa. An empty chicken bucket sat on the coffee table, and Gladys saw board game pieces on the floor.

"Gladys?" her mom's voice called. Gladys tiptoed to the sofa, and her mom rubbed the sleep from her eyes. "How was the party?"

"It was great," Gladys said honestly. "The best one I've ever been to."

"I'm so glad." Her mom smiled. Gladys's dad let out a snorty kind of snore. "I think that means that Dad is glad, too," her mom whispered, and she and Gladys both giggled.

"You should head up to bed," her mom continued, but as she said it she scooted forward and reached an arm around the waist of Gladys's purple dress, pulling her closer. "I'm really proud of you for making new friends," she murmured. "I know that it's not easy to do."

Gladys didn't know what to say, so she just gave her mom a kiss on the cheek. Her mom smiled, then closed her eyes and let her head roll back against the sofa cushion.

Gladys carried an afghan over from the recliner and smoothed it onto her sleeping parents' legs. Then she switched off the hallway light and felt her way up the staircase in the dark.

It was past noon when Gladys woke up the next day. She was eager to get to work writing her review, but was also dying to talk to Sandy. She checked the window, but didn't see him in his room; she'd have to call him. Still in her pajamas (her favorite spring ones, with strawberries all over them), Gladys hurried down the stairs—and found both of her parents sitting in the kitchen, waiting for her.

"Good afternoon, sleepyhead," her dad said. "Notice anything different in here?"

Gladys looked around the room. She saw the same old toaster, the same old microwave, the same old fridge with its same old Approved and Unapproved Activities lists. But then her eyes came to the window . . .

"You got new curtains!"

Gladys's mom rose from her seat and walked over to the window. "We picked them up this morning, while you were sleeping. And they're not just *any* curtains," she said. "Come here, feel them."

Gladys walked over and rubbed the material between her fingers. The curtains were a drab gray color with tiny orange flecks, and the fabric felt sort of rubbery to the touch.

"Um, interesting," Gladys said. They definitely weren't as pretty as the old curtains, which had been blue-and-white chiffon. In fact, Gladys thought, if Charissa were here, she would probably call these new curtains "hideous."

"They're *flameproof*," Gladys's mom announced happily.

"Oh!" Gladys said, though she wasn't really sure why her mom seemed so excited about this. Her parents hardly ever cooked with the stove, much less with a blowtorch, so the chance of their ever causing a kitchen fire seemed small.

"Gladdy, come sit down," her dad said. Still confused, Gladys took a seat. Her mom followed suit.

"We got a phone call from your teacher yesterday, while you were at Sandy's," he said.

"You did?" Gladys asked.

"Yes," her mom said. "Remember, she wanted to talk to us after Parents' Night, but there wasn't time?"

Gladys's dad pushed his glasses up on his nose. "Gladdy, why didn't you tell us about winning that essay contest?"

"I didn't win the whole contest," Gladys said quickly. "I was just the winner for my class. I didn't think it was a big deal."

"Well," her mom said, scratching at a spot of dried pizza sauce on the table, "Ms. Quincy says that you're a very talented writer, and that your essay showed a real passion for cooking. She even read it to us over the phone."

"She did?" Gladys cringed slightly. Her essay went into a lot of detail about her secret cooking projects.

"She did," her dad said. "And, well, it got us thinking about your punishment."

*Uh-oh,* Gladys thought. What would they use this time to make sure she stayed out of the kitchen— surveillance cameras? Heat sensors?

"First of all, the curtains are paid off," he continued, "so we have no more reason to hold back your allowance."

"Uh-huh," Gladys said miserably. Who cared if she had money to spend if she was about to get banned from the kitchen for life?

"And secondly, we told you that you needed to have some fun, to do more normal activities for a kid your age. And, well—you've done a terrific job with that."

"I have?" Gladys thought of the list on the fridge. She hadn't thrown a single snowball, or been to the mall even one time.

"Don't think that we haven't been paying attention," Gladys's mom said. "It's wonderful that you and Sandy have become so close, but now you've got Parm and Charissa, too! From zero friends to three in three months—that's very impressive, honey! Now, tell the truth. Isn't it nice to have friends?"

"Yeah," Gladys admitted. She still missed cooking most of the time, but it was definitely good to have other kids to talk to—especially when she needed help making new desserts or planning secret missions into New York City.

"Well, you've proven that you can have a normal social life," her dad said. "So the real question now is, can you balance that with your passion?"

"My passion?" Gladys said. "What do you mean?"

"Something else is different about this kitchen," her mom announced with a smile. "It's small, so you probably didn't notice it the first time. Go ahead, take another look around."

Slowly, Gladys scraped her chair back and stood up. She took a few tentative steps around the kitchen. Same old toaster. Same old microwave. Same old fridge with its same old Approved and Unapproved . . .

Wait.

Gladys looked closer at the two lists. A word had been crossed out on the Unapproved list and added to the bottom of the Approved list.

*Cooking.*

Gladys let out a squeak and turned back to face her parents. They were beaming.

"There are still some rules!" Gladys's mom said quickly as Gladys barreled into her with a hug. "You're not allowed to cook alone—there always has to be someone to help you so things don't get out of hand!"

"That's right," her dad chimed in. "Even real chefs have sous-chefs to help them out."

Gladys gaped at her father. "How do you know that word?" He'd pronounced the word more like *sauce* than the correct *sue*—but still, she was impressed.

He reddened slightly. "I looked it up online. Turns out your tablet has all sorts of cool cooking apps! Anyway, it's French for 'assistant to the chef,' right?"

Gladys threw her arms around him, too.

"And any cooking you do cannot take time away from schoolwork or from hanging out with your new friends," her mom continued. "Agreed?"

Gladys nodded vigorously. Yesterday may have been the best day of her life, but this was turning into a close second.

Ironically, in the week that followed, Gladys had no time for cooking at all. She had a review to write, homework to do, and friends who insisted on hearing all about her adventure in the city.

Sandy called her that afternoon. "Gatsby, I've been waiting all day for the news!" he said. "How did it go? Did the plan work?"

"The plan?" Gladys laughed. "Which plan?" Then, making sure that her parents were far enough away in the living room that they couldn't hear her, she told him the whole story.

At school on Monday, Parm cornered Gladys in the

hallway before class and demanded to know how the trip to Classy Cakes had gone. Speaking as quietly as she could, Gladys filled her in.

"Well, it's too bad you had to eat all of those disgusting desserts," Parm said when Gladys finally finished. "But I suppose that's what a professional does. You really pulled it off!" And she gave Gladys a hearty slap on the back. It hurt a bit, but Gladys didn't complain—she knew it was the same kind of slap Parm gave her soccer teammates when they scored a goal, and it made her feel good.

During lunch, everyone else wanted to hear all about Charissa's birthday party in the city. Charissa was more than happy to provide detailed descriptions of the limo, the musical, and the desserts, and Gladys was more than happy to let Charissa do all the talking. By the end of the day, most people seemed to forget that Gladys had even been along for the ride.

But Charissa hadn't. She caught up with Gladys at the bike rack after school. "Gladys!" she cried. "Omigosh, wasn't Saturday so *fun*? I keep thinking about that tree-nut tart. Do you think you could find a recipe for it?"

"Probably," Gladys said. "Although I'm not sure I have the right kind of pan at home."

"Whatever," Charissa said with a wave of her hand. "My parents own every kitchen utensil ever invented, so we'll just make it at my house. Maybe Thursday?

Oh, wait, Thursday is horseback. Maybe Sunday? Oh, wait, that's my dance recital. Let me check my activities calendar and get back to you, okay?"

"Okay," Gladys said. She half expected Charissa to forget all about this by tomorrow, but if she didn't . . . well, the Bentleys lived in a very nice house, and Gladys wouldn't mind having access to their kitchen! Plus, when she was in a good, stuffed-with-dessert mood, Charissa could be almost fun to hang out with.

"It's a date," Gladys said. "Or, a date for a date."

"Don't say *date*!" Charissa squealed. "It just makes me hungry for that sticky date pudding from Classy Cakes!"

Gladys worked on her review every day after school that week, and finally e-mailed it to Fiona Inglethorpe on Saturday. Once she clicked "Send," Gladys felt a lightness flood through her, like she was a marshmallow bobbing in a sea of Mrs. Anderson's cinnamon hot chocolate. She'd done it! She had written a restaurant review for the *New York Standard*! She would have liked to bake a cake to celebrate, but since she hadn't found time to stock up on ingredients at Mr. Eng's yet, she settled for simply dancing around the house.

Fiona e-mailed her back on Monday. She made some small corrections, but overall she loved the review. It would run that Wednesday in the Dining section.

And just to confirm, Fiona wrote, Gladys Gatsby is the by-line you use? No middle initial or anything?

Gladys had to do a Web search to find a definition for *byline,* and was a little embarrassed when she found out that it was literally just the line in the article that said "*by*" and the author's name. She was about to write back that "Gladys Gatsby" was fine when she remembered a conversation she'd had with Sandy weeks ago about her parents.

Dear Ms. Inglethorpe,

I'm so glad you liked the review. For my byline, I would prefer to use "G. Gatsby." Thank you!

Sincerely,
Gladys

Gladys wasn't sure what the protocol was for choosing your byline, but she hoped that the editor would honor her request. That way, if by some small chance someone *did* show the review to her parents, or anyone else she knew, they wouldn't know she had written it. The writer could be named Greg Gatsby, or Geraldine Gatsby. There had to be other Gatsbys in New York.

# Chapter 30

# JUST DESSERTS

THE FOLLOWING REVIEW APPEARED ON the front page of the *New York Standard*'s Dining section that Wednesday.

### JUST DESSERTS
by G. GATSBY

Do you want to go to Classy Cakes, Midtown Manhattan's new all-dessert bistro? You'd better start planning your visit early. First of all, there is a week-long wait for reservations—and good luck getting a table without one.

If you do get in, congratulations! Now it's time to start saving your pennies, because cake prices start at $12.50 a slice.

Once you're through the door, the waiters and waitresses, dressed in yellow and black, buzz busily around the dining room. But the real problem is the hostess, who reigns over the restaurant like a mean queen bee. So it's a good thing that the desserts are delicious—so delicious that the moment the first bite touches your taste buds, you'll forget all about the trouble, and the expense, and the rudeness.

Chef Allison Sconestein-Alforno has created a dessert for every kind of appetite. If you like pecan pie, then you'll love her tree-nut tart, which adds fancy nut varieties like black walnuts, Marcona almonds, and DuChilly hazelnuts to the mix. But if you're in the mood for something creamier, you can choose from among the lemon-lavender, mocha-mint, and berry-basil custards, where fresh herbs add the perfect kick to the classic custard flavors.

For a dessert that's as filling as a whole meal, you can try the belly-swelling ginger-sultana bread pudding or the mouth-gluingly gooey sticky date pudding. Kids will beg their parents for the homemade ice creams in cookie flavors, like cinnamon graham and banana biscuit, which can be served on their own or sundae-style (ask for an extra squirt of the maple whipped cream!). And if things get too sweet for you, you can always order a cheese plate—its many colors make it almost as pretty as it is stinky.

But the restaurant is called Classy Cakes, so you probably want to hear about those $12.50 cake slices. Layered high on their plates, they're as tall and teetering as a lady in high-heeled shoes, but feel as moist in your mouth as the Amazon rain forest on a rainy day. Their flavors will send your taste buds on a trip around the world: the Moroccan cake features pistachio and cardamom, the Chinese cake has green tea and sesame seeds, and the Belgian cake has chocolate and . . . well, more chocolate.

The creative cakes will probably be many diners' favorite desserts, but for me, the most impressive item on the menu was one of the most traditional: the crème brûlée. It's hard to explain what, exactly, made this dessert so special, so I'll just say that Ms. Sconestein-Alforno—or one of her sous-chefs— is much more skilled with a blowtorch than this reviewer will ever be.

### ★★★★ (a delectable dining experience)

Mr. Eng had the Dining section spread open on the counter when Gladys walked in that morning. She'd biked over on her way to school—*just to get a croissant,* she told herself. But really, she was dying to get a look at the paper.

"Good morning, Mr. Eng," she said.

"Good morning, Gladys," he said with a smile. "Hey, the herb in that berry-basil custard—was it Thai basil or sweet basil?"

"I'm pretty sure it was sweet—" Gladys started without thinking. Then she felt herself turning very red.

Mr. Eng chuckled and slapped the newspaper. "I knew it!" he cried—and then, more quietly, said, "Don't worry, your secret's safe with me." He promised to save her five copies of the paper, which she could come pick up after school.

Aside from Mr. Eng, only two other adults in East Dumpsford read the review. One was Sandy's mom, who flipped through the paper as she took a break from coding a new website at home. *Ooh, desserts!* she thought when she saw the headline. Then, like most readers, she jumped right into the article. If she glanced at the byline at all, she probably thought it said "G. Gadfly"—short for "Gilbert Gadfly," the paper's regular critic—rather than "G. Gatsby." In fact, thousands of readers in the tristate area made this mistake, and then raved that this was the best review Gilbert Gadfly had written in a long time.

The last reader also didn't notice the byline when she sat down at a table in the teachers' lounge with

her mug of green tea. But once she started reading—
and enjoying the writer's creative metaphors—she
couldn't keep the smile off her face. There was only
one person Violetta Quincy knew who wrote about
food with such passion, and when she finished the
article and finally looked closely at the byline, her
suspicions were confirmed.

It looked like her student hadn't lost the *New York
Standard* essay contest after all.

That evening, Gladys and Sandy sat on the floor in
the Rabbit Room, reading through Gladys's review
for the third time. They had already raided both of
their houses for an envelope and stamps so Gladys
could mail a copy to Paris. Aunt Lydia, she was sure,
would not only keep her secret, but would be very
proud. Another three copies were stashed carefully
away under the pajamas in Gladys's dresser drawer
at home, but she couldn't bring herself to hide the last
one away—not yet.

"You did it!" Sandy said.

"*We* did it," Gladys corrected him. "I couldn't have
done it without you."

"Sure you could've."

"Nope. Could not."

Edward Hopper leaped over Sandy's outstretched
leg like he was doing rabbit hurdles, and Dennis Hopper reached his twitching nose up to the corner of the

newspaper Gladys was holding. Remembering how attached the fat rabbit had been to the last Dining section he came in contact with, Gladys snatched it away from him.

"So," Sandy said, "what's your next assignment?"

"What do you mean?" Gladys asked.

"For the *Standard*," Sandy said. "Haven't they given you another review to do yet?"

"Yet?" Gladys cried, folding up her paper. "I just finished this one!"

"Yeah," said Sandy, "but you're their new star critic! They've got to give you more reviews!"

Gladys didn't even want to think about how she might sneak back into the city for another assignment.

"I may need to take a vacation from reviewing," Gladys said. "You know, concentrate on not failing the sixth grade."

"Yeah, well," Sandy huffed, "we'll see what Fiona says."

Two days later, this e-mail came through from Fiona.

Dear Gladys,

Thank you again for your great work on the Classy Cakes review. I think that your writing is a breath of fresh air for the *New York Standard,* and I hope that you'll continue to write for us.

Our regular critic, Mr. Gadfly, has recovered and is back at work, so I don't have any freelance assignments at the moment—but I'm sure that I will this summer, when several new restaurants are slated to open. Meanwhile, have a great spring!

Best,
Fiona Inglethorpe


Spring had, indeed, arrived in New York.

In Manhattan, Fiona wandered through the greenmarket, buying up armloads of deep pink rhubarb stalks to bake into pies and pale pink cherry blossoms to decorate her table.

At East Dumpsford Elementary, kids hung their coats on the fence while they ran around at recess, and the intrepid Owen Green—"crazy Owen Green," scoffed Parm—showed up at school in shorts.

Gladys, meanwhile, finally found time to shop at Mr. Eng's that Saturday, and even convinced her parents to forego their weekly trip to the Super Dump-Mart and come along. At first her mom was intimidated by the fridge full of high-fat cheeses, and her dad eyed the price list at the butcher counter warily. But Mr. Eng won them both over with free samples of his latest delivery: the first local asparagus of the season, which he had roasted simply with olive oil and salt.

"It's delicious!" Gladys's mom cried, helping herself to a third stalk.

Gladys's dad agreed. "I didn't know vegetables could taste this good."

They ended up buying four bunches, and even let Gladys pick out a bottle of fancy olive oil to cook them in at home.

When they got back to the house, Gladys and her dad unloaded the groceries while her mom opened the front door and took in the mail. She was at the dining room table, opening envelopes, when they came in with the bags. "Junk," she said, tossing one letter aside and ripping into another. "Junk . . . bill . . . junk . . ." But then she stopped, squinting hard at the paper she had just pulled out of the last envelope.

"George," she said finally, "come look at this."

Gladys's dad set his bag down and went to look at the paper in his wife's hand. He stared at it for a moment, then picked up the envelope, then looked back at the paper. Finally he looked up at Gladys.

"Gladdy," he said, "why has the *New York Standard* sent you a check for a thousand dollars?"

*Fuuudge,* thought Gladys. Her goose was cooked now.

## Acknowledgments

THIS BOOK TOOK ALMOST A DECADE TO "COOK," AND would probably still be simmering on a back burner if it wasn't for the following people:

Ammi-Joan Paquette, my brilliant agent and fellow foodie, who believed in this story and matched it with the perfect editor;

Shauna Rossano, who is that editor, and whose insight has made this book so much richer than I ever imagined possible;

Kelly Murphy, whose scrumptious cover art has brought Gladys's world to life;

Everyone else at Penguin Young Readers Group who has helped bring *All Four Stars* out into the world;

Katharine Davis Reich, Jessica Wells-Hasan, Evelyn Chen, Miriam Schiffer, and Allison Brennan—the Bread-basket Writers' Group—who nourished this book from its first paragraph (and its author with love and peanut butter pies);

Eugene Myers, who cheerfully shared everything he knew about breaking into children's publishing, and Julie Sloane for putting us in touch;

Authoress, proprietor of the Miss Snark's First Victim blog, and Jodi Meadows, who plucked the first page of this story from the slush and got it in front of my agent;

Malini Mukhopadhyay, who taught me so much about Indian cooking and culture (and who was the first person, way back in college, to insist that I check out that new *Harry Potter* series);

The Dartmouth College Department of English and Creative Writing—and particularly Ernest Hebert and Cleopatra Mathis—who fostered my love of literature and gave me the confidence to try creating some of my own;

My many friends and fellow writers who read drafts of this manuscript and provided feedback and encouragement at crucial points: Hoi Ning Ngai, Christine Percheski, Nomi Stone, Catherine Bridle, Merrie Morris, Katie Wade, Lauren Sabel, Cindy Strandvold, Ann Bedichek, Jessica Lawson, Krista Van Dolzer, Joy McCullough-Carranza, Lisa Ann O'Kane, Sarah Hilbert and Mónica Bustamante Wagner;

My EMLA family (the "Gango"), and especially my fellow bloggers at EMU's Debuts, who with their collective awesomeness have convinced me that kids' authors really are the best people in the world;

My writing students—Emily, Lucia, and Evelyn Paul, and Aksel, Max, and Oskar Moe—who clamored to read this book as soon as they found out I'd written it and quickly became Gladys's best "real-world" friends;

The Cahills and Campbells—Mollie, Sarah, Jim, Heidi,

and Matt—who have welcomed me into their clan with endless love, support, and square donuts;

My aunt, Judy Gruber, who took me on adventures into Manhattan as a toddler and, many years later, stayed up all night reading the first full draft of this book;

My parents, Barbara and Fred Dairman, who taught me the subtleties of microwave cooking and have been cheering me on in my writing pursuits for decades now;

My sister, Brooke Robyn Dairman, who inspires me to continue pursuing my creative dreams by never giving up on hers;

And finally, Andy Cahill, who in a thousand different ways every day makes my existence a happy one.

# GAJAR KA HALWA (Carrot Pudding)

## makes 4 cups—about 8 servings

Like carrot cake? Then you'll love this sweet carrot pudding, which is a specialty of the Punjab region of India and Pakistan. Even picky Parm can't resist it!

<u>Note</u>: Traditionally, this recipe is made with ghee (clarified butter, available at Indian grocery stores), but if you don't have any, you can substitute regular butter.

# Ingredients:

<u>Nut-and-raisin topping</u>:
- 1 Tbsp ghee or butter
- 2 Tbsp cashews (halved or chopped)
- 2 Tbsp almonds (sliced, slivered, or chopped)
- 2 Tbsp raisins

<u>Carrot pudding</u>:
- 4 Tbsp ghee or butter
- 10–12 carrots, peeled and shredded
- 3 cups milk (at least 1%, and the higher in fat the better)
- ½ cup sugar (plus more to taste)
- 1 tsp ground cardamom

# Instructions:

If you are a young chef, ask an adult to work with you on this recipe.

In a large, deep skillet (preferably nonstick), melt 1 Tbsp ghee or butter over medium heat. Add the cashews and almonds and toast until the nuts are golden brown and fragrant, 4–5 minutes. Add the raisins for the last minute and cook, stirring, until they are plumped but not burnt. Remove the nuts and raisins into a bowl and set aside.

Melt the remaining 4 Tbsp ghee or butter in the skillet. Sautee the shredded carrots in the fat for 3–5 minutes. Add the milk and bring the mixture to a simmer. Cook, stirring occasionally, until the milk is all evaporated, about 1 hour.

Stir in the sugar and cardamom and cook for another 3 or 4 minutes, until the sugar is melted and well incorporated. Taste and add more sugar as desired. Before serving, stir in the nuts and raisins, or sprinkle them on top of the pudding.

Serve warm, at room temperature, or cold in small bowls (a little goes a long way).

# "BLUEBARB" (Blueberry-Rhubarb) CRUMBLE
## serves 4–6

Together, blueberries and rhubarb make a delicious sweet-and-sour filling for pies, cobblers, and crumbles. If, like Gladys, you need to impress someone with an unusual dessert, give this one a try—just make sure you save some for yourself, too!

<u>Note</u>: You can use fresh or frozen fruit in this recipe.

# Ingredients:

<u>Filling</u>:
> 2½ cups rhubarb, diced
> 3 cups blueberries, rinsed
> ½ cup sugar
> 3 Tbsp tapioca starch or cornstarch
> 2 Tbsp lemon juice
> ¼ tsp cinnamon

<u>Topping</u>:
> ¼ cup walnuts
> ½ cup brown sugar
> ½ cup flour
> ½ tsp cinnamon
> 4 Tbsp cold butter, cut into bits
> 1 Tbsp neutral-tasting oil, such as canola
> ½ cup rolled oats
> salt

<u>Optional garnish</u>:
> vanilla ice cream

# Instructions:

If you are a young chef, ask an adult to work with you on this recipe. Preheat the oven to 350° F.

In a large bowl, combine all of the filling ingredients. Toss to mix everything well, then transfer the mixture to a loaf pan.

In a food processor, pulse the walnuts, brown sugar, flour, a pinch of salt, and cinnamon together a few times until the walnuts have been broken into smaller pieces. Add the butter bits and oil and process until the mixture has a uniform, crumbly texture. Add the rolled oats and pulse 10 times, until the oats are incorporated but are still mostly whole.

Spread the topping over the fruit in the loaf pan, covering it evenly. Bake for 30 minutes. (You might need a few extra minutes if you used frozen fruit.)

Let the crumble cool a bit before serving, either on its own or topped with vanilla ice cream.

TURN THE PAGE FOR A TEASER OF
GLADYS'S SUMMER CAMP SEQUEL,

# BITTER BIRTHDAY

GLADYS GATSBY'S TWELFTH BIRTHDAY should have been her happiest one yet.

She was at a fabulous new restaurant in Manhattan on an outing she'd been planning for weeks. Back at home, a three-tiered, strawberry-lime birthday cake (which, of course, Gladys had baked herself) was waiting to be eaten. And best of all, Gladys's parents had allowed her to invite her friends along for the festivities. A year ago, Gladys hadn't had any friends to invite to a birthday party—but now she had three, and they were all here at Fusión Tapas with her.

Too bad they weren't speaking to one another.

Gladys glanced around the table. Parm Singh's thick black eyebrows knit into an angry scrunch as she scowled alternately at Charissa Bentley and Sandy Anderson. Next to her, Charissa was flicking her high brown ponytail over her shoulder about ten times a minute, shooting sneers in Sandy's or Parm's direction each time. And Sandy—whose round cheeks were flushed almost as red as the bottle of spicy sauce in the middle of the table—had scooted his chair so far away from both girls that he was now practically sitting in Gladys's dad's lap.

All this bitterness, and they hadn't even gotten their food yet!

The evening had started off much more smoothly, with the Gatsbys piling into their station wagon to drive into the city. "Hey, I don't remember agreeing to throw a party like this," Gladys's dad had joked as he turned the key in the ignition. "Gladdy, I knew that hanging around with that Bentley girl was going to give you big ideas."

Gladys smiled. It was true that she'd gotten the idea to spend her birthday at a restaurant in the city from Charissa, who'd brought Gladys into Manhattan on a birthday outing just three months earlier. But Gladys's ulterior motive had nothing to do with wanting to be popular like Charissa.

It had everything to do with her top secret job as a restaurant critic for New York City's biggest newspaper.

It wasn't a job she had even meant to apply for, but a few months back, Gladys's entry for the *New York Standard* sixth-grade essay contest had somehow ended up on the desk of Fiona Inglethorpe, chief editor of the *Standard*'s Dining section. Fiona must have liked what she read—and must have assumed that Gladys was a professional adult writer—because she had e-mailed Gladys with a reviewing assignment for the paper.

Almost overnight, Gladys had morphed from a regular sixth-grader into a sort of foodie secret agent. She couldn't let her editor know her age, or she'd get in trouble for being too young. She couldn't let the restaurants find out she was a critic, or they'd give her special treatment, trying to influence her reviews. And, most important, she couldn't let her parents know about her new job. These days, they only let her indulge her love of cooking at home because they thought she spent the rest of her time being a "normal kid." If they found out that she *actually* spent most of her free time writing about food for the country's most important newspaper . . . well, she could kiss those kitchen privileges good-bye forever.

So Gladys's parents didn't know that she'd chosen this restaurant for her birthday dinner because she needed to review it for next week's Dining section. But Sandy did, and since he lived next door, he was the first of her friends to join them. Jogging up to their car, he looked different than usual: He wore pressed khaki pants instead of shorts, and his usually mussed-up blond hair had been sculpted with gel into a severe wave. But underneath all that was the same old Sandy.

"Happy birthday, Gatsby!" He fist-bumped her as he climbed into the car, then shoved a wrapped package into her lap. "Hey, Mr. and Mrs. Gatsby, thanks for having me. This is gonna be excellent—I can't wait to try the tapas!"

He was overplaying things a little, Gladys thought, but her mom seemed to buy it. Swiveling around in her seat, she beamed at him. Gladys's mom thought that having an active social life was very important, so she grinned at just about everything that came out of Gladys's friends' mouths—even if it was enthusiasm for tiny plates of Spanish-inspired cuisine.

"You're very welcome, Sandy," she said. "We're just thrilled to have you along."

"You've got your notebook?" Sandy whispered as the car turned onto Landfill View Road. Gladys gave him a tiny nod and patted her dress pocket. Inside were the materials she needed to carry off her secret mission: a tiny reviewing journal and two sharp golf pencils.

"And you've got the charts?" Gladys whispered back. She and Sandy had spent the last week—every day since summer vacation had begun—at his house, scouring the Fusión Tapas menu online and plotting who should order what. The menu featured eighteen different dishes, so if Gladys wanted to taste them all, every person in their party would have to order three different things. Luckily, "tapas" were small plates, so Gladys knew that the portions wouldn't be huge.

Sandy nodded and slid two folded-up printouts out of his pocket. Gladys quickly stuffed them into her journal. She and Sandy already had their orders memorized, as did Parm, who also knew about Gladys's secret work for the *Standard*. As for the other diners, Gladys had been dropping hints about what they should order all week and hoped she'd planted seeds in their minds: seeds that would grow into roasted asparagus for her mom, fried eggplant for her dad, and stuffed peppers for Charissa.

Soon the Gatsbys' car pulled into the Singhs' driveway. Parm stepped outside wearing a beautiful salwar kameez of green chiffon, but she kept her head tucked down as though she were embarrassed. When Sandy pushed open the back door, she grabbed a fistful of her flowing pants and nearly vaulted into the far backseat.

"Happy birthday, Gladys," she said, handing over a small gift bag tied shut with a curl of ribbon. "And sorry about . . . this." She glanced down at her outfit. "My mom looked at the restaurant's website, and when she saw how fancy it is, she made me dress up."

"That's okay," Gladys said, pointing to her own striped sundress. "Mine did, too, see? Anyway, you look really nice."

"Yeah," Sandy chimed in. "You look like a princess!"

Parm's eyes narrowed. *Uh-oh*, Gladys thought. That was definitely the wrong thing to say to a girl who spent most of recess either kicking around a soccer ball or punching Owen Green.

Sandy, though, seemed oblivious to Parm's glare. "I'm Sandy, by the way," he said. "Sandy Anderson. Maybe your parents know my mom? She teaches at East Dumpsford Yoga, and she studied in India."

"Well, if she studied there, then she *must* have met my parents," Parm said witheringly. "It's not like there's over *a billion people* in India or anything."

Sandy twisted to look at Gladys, a bewildered expression on his face. "I thought she was supposed to be the nice one," he muttered.

Gladys couldn't think of how to respond. Sandy went to a private school, so he had never met Gladys's other friends. But if Sandy and Parm already weren't getting along, then adding Charissa to the mix definitely wasn't going to help.

And just as she suspected, Gladys heard both of her friends groan audibly as Charissa flounced down her front walk five minutes later. She wore an elaborate red dress trimmed in black lace and matching high heels, and carried an enormous present wrapped in shiny gold paper.

"Is she wearing *gloves*?" Parm asked incredulously. "It's eighty degrees outside!"

Gladys looked closer and saw that Charissa *was* wearing gloves, though they were black lace ones with no fingertips, so she was pretty sure they were meant to be fashionable rather than warm.

"Maybe temperatures are cooler in The Seabreeze," Sandy said. The Seabreeze—East Dumpsford's most exclusive waterfront neighborhood—was where the Bentleys' large house was located.

"Right—not like sweltering, overpopulated India," Parm snapped.

"Dude, I didn't say anything about India!"

"Cool it, you guys," Gladys begged—but before she could say more, the car door flew open.

"*Hola!*" Charissa squealed. She dropped her huge gift on the floor, threw her arms around Gladys, and planted a lipsticky kiss on each of her cheeks. "*That's* how they say hello in Spain," she informed everyone as she climbed in. "And this is what they wear. Or what flamenco dancers wear, at least." She smoothed the skirt of her dress with one of her gloves. "Since we're going to a Spanish restaurant, I thought it would be the perfect outfit. I had Mommy order it specially for me from Madrid!"

"How thoughtful of you, Charissa!" Gladys's mother exclaimed. It was no secret that Gladys's mom liked Charissa the best of Gladys's friends, possibly more than Gladys even liked her. Charissa loved to be the center of attention and tell everyone what to do—traits that made her pretty much Gladys's opposite. But they had one important thing in common: They both loved good food, and could talk about it for hours on end. Gladys wasn't sure yet that she could trust Charissa with her restaurant-reviewing secret, but if she was going to a fancy restaurant, she knew she wanted Charissa with her.

As the station wagon merged onto the highway, Sandy gawked at Charissa's dress. Gladys couldn't blame him; it gleamed like fluorescent strawberry juice, even in the low light of the car.

Charissa eyed Sandy coolly. "You know it's rude to stare, right?"

"Sorry," he mumbled.

Charissa pursed her brightly colored lips, and Gladys felt sure that she was about to chew him out. But instead she said, "That's okay. You're Gladys's little friend—Sandy, right?" She shot him an indulgent smile. "I wouldn't expect someone *so* much younger than the rest of us to know about proper manners."

"I—what?" Sandy spluttered. "I'm only a year younger than you!"

"Yes," Charissa continued, "but boys are less mature than girls to start. So an eleven-year-old boy is really the equivalent of, like, an eight-year-old girl. Don't you think, Parm?"

"I'm staying out of this," Parm said.

Gladys had to jump in. "Sandy's very mature," she

assured Charissa. "Like an adult sometimes, really. You should see some of the computer games he's designed!"

Sandy gave Gladys a small smile of thanks.

"Well, Gladys," Charissa drawled, "it's your birthday, and he's your friend, so of course you're right. I'll say no more."

And she didn't. In fact, nobody did all the way into Manhattan—not even Gladys's mom, though in her case it may have been due to nerves. Unlike Gladys's dad, who took the train into Manhattan every day for work, her mom hardly ever ventured into New York City. She said that the tall buildings made her feel claustrophobic, and she worried about pickpockets. In fact, she had left her purse at home and insisted that Gladys's dad take only his driver's license and a single debit card on the birthday outing to help limit their losses in case of a violent holdup.

"This is completely unnecessary," her dad had grumbled as he emptied his wallet onto the kitchen table. But he'd given in to avoid starting the night off with a fight.

As everyone lined up in the entryway to Fusión Tapas, Gladys hoped that her friends wouldn't be fighting all night. She had a job to do, after all, and she was going to need them to work together to pull it off.

Sandy was standing closest to her, so she decided

to check in with him first. "Which three tapas will you be ordering again?" she whispered.

"The calamari, the potato omelet, and whatever special number two is," he whispered back. According to the restaurant's website, it always served two specials in addition to the regular menu, so Gladys had planned to order one of them and have Sandy—her least finicky friend—order the other. "Don't worry, Gatsby," he assured her. "I've got this."

She nodded; no matter what else happened, she knew she could rely on Sandy. Gladys turned to check in with Parm next, but found Charissa standing in her way.

"Gladys, do you know what you're going to get?" she asked excitedly. "I've been studying the menu online all week! I have to get the smoked almonds; that's a given."

Gladys had assumed this—since she knew how much Charissa liked nuts—so it was already filled in on the ordering chart. And as for the other two slots next to Charissa's name . . .

"How about the stuffed piquillo peppers," Gladys suggested, "and maybe the goose kebabs?"

Charissa's button nose wrinkled. "I don't know," she said. "Isn't goose really greasy? I wouldn't want to get stains on my dress."

"Right," Gladys said, doing some quick calculations in her head. Maybe *she* could order the goose and let

Charissa have the griddled polenta cakes that were next to her own name on the chart. "Well, how about the—"

Just then, something slammed into Gladys's shoulder—hard. It was Parm. "Stupid sandals," she muttered. "Sorry. I never trip in my cleats."

"So, Parm," Charissa said, tossing her ponytail over her shoulder, "what are you going to order? I thought you didn't eat anything other than, like, plain spaghetti."

Gladys felt Parm's body stiffen and hoped her friend remembered the answer they had practiced in case this question came up. In truth, Parm was the pickiest eater Gladys knew; she ate a couple of things besides spaghetti, but not much, and certainly nothing that would be found on the menu of a Spanish restaurant.

"In honor of Gladys's birthday, I'm going to be adventurous," Parm recited. "I'm going to try some new dishes and hope to be pleasantly surprised."

Gladys gave Parm's pinkie a grateful squeeze. She felt confident now that Parm remembered her role, too: keep track of what everyone else orders, and then order whatever is left on the menu. Gladys knew Parm had no intention of putting even one morsel of tapas into her mouth, so it really didn't matter what she ordered in the end.

"Gladys Jane?" the maître d' called out. "Party of six?"

Gladys's hand shot into the air. "That's us!" Thankfully, her parents had allowed her to make the dinner reservations, and she'd been careful not to give the restaurant her last name, since she published her reviews under the byline "G. Gatsby." But as the maître d' swept them off to their table in the middle of the loud, mirror-paneled dining room, Gladys couldn't help but worry. There were still so many moving parts to her plan.

Soon they were all seated at a round table covered with a funky turquoise tablecloth. Ice clinked in their skinny water glasses as they perused the menu, and the waiter came by a few minutes later to recite the specials. "We have some lovely steamed lobsterrr claws today, serrrved with frrresh dill-infused butterrr sauce." He rolled his *r*'s so forcefully that, next to Gladys, Sandy giggled. "And, forrr a second special, we have the chef's homemade rrrabbit sausage, gently charrred and serrrrved atop a stew of fava beans."

Sandy stopped laughing, and Gladys immediately knew why. He had two pet rabbits at home, Edward and Dennis Hopper, and rabbit meat was possibly the only food on earth he wouldn't eat.

"Arrre we rrready to orrrderrr?" the waiter asked. "I hearrr we have a birrrthday girrrl?" He turned to Gladys, his grin wide beneath a pencil-thin mustache.

Gladys froze. Should she stick with the original plan and order the lobster, special number one? Or should she order the rabbit special for herself and hope that Sandy got the hint and switched with her? But would Sandy ever talk to her again if she ate rabbit right in front of him?

"Um . . . I . . ." Gladys looked frantically around the table, but that only added to her confusion. What was Charissa going to decide on—the goose or the polenta? And what about her parents??

"Perrrhaps you need anotherrr minute," the waiter trilled, and relief washed over Gladys as he backed away. It would be easier if she could place her order near the end.

"Well, I know what I'd like," Gladys's mother said, and the waiter turned eagerly back toward their table. "The beef-filled baguette—that's like a hamburger, right? I'll try that. And these olive-oil-crisped potato wedges—that sounds sort of like French fries. Oh, and the ham-wrapped roasted asparagus." She shot Gladys a wink. Gladys was pretty sure her mom had never tasted asparagus until the day Gladys had practically forced her to try a sample at Mr. Eng's Gourmet Grocery. But now that she knew she liked it, she ate it all the time. *Good job, Mom,* Gladys thought. *Maybe we'll try Brussels sprouts next.*

"Everything my wife mentioned sounds good," Gladys's dad said, shutting his menu with a decisive *clap!* "I'll have the same."

"No!" The word flew out of Gladys's mouth before

she could stop herself. In an instant, all the heads at her table—and several tables around them—swung in her direction.

*Fudge,* she thought. Rule number one of restaurant reviewing was *not* to make a spectacle of yourself. Staying unnoticed and anonymous was the best way to avoid exposing your identity.

But now everyone was staring at her, so she had to say something. "Remember how we talked about this, Dad?" she said. "About how we were all going to order different stuff tonight? That way, we can share and all get to try more new things!"

"That was a nice idea, Gladdy," her dad started, "but I'm afraid that there just aren't many other things on this menu that appeal—"

"*Excuse me.*" Charissa was now rising from her seat. "If Gladys wants everyone to order different things, then that's what we should do. A girl's birthday is *not* the time to say no to her. Is it, Mr. Gatsby?" Charissa flashed her teeth at him in a way that seemed to be half smiling, half threatening to eat him alive.

Gladys's dad's eyes widened, and for a second, it looked like he might tell Charissa that he could say no to his daughter anytime he darn well chose. But then his hands betrayed him by slipping the menu back open across his plate.

"Well, I . . . I guess I could try the fried eggplant . . .

and, um, the chorizo sausage . . . and the gazpacho. Please," he added meekly.

Charissa retook her seat, and Sandy leaned over toward Gladys's ear. "Okay," he whispered. "I guess I can see why you brought her."

Things got a little easier after that. Sandy placed his order, substituting the lobster special for the rabbit, and gave Gladys a look that made it clear that her ordering rabbit would *not* be okay with him. Charissa picked the polenta over the goose, so Gladys got the goose, the octopus, and the sliced pork loin. That meant that when Parm's turn came, there were only two items left on the regular menu that hadn't been mentioned yet. She dutifully ordered them from the waiter, then glanced over toward Gladys. "Should I get that other special, too?"

"No, that's okay," Gladys said—she would just have to leave the rabbit out of her review. She turned to the waiter again and said, "But would it be possible to get a small bowl of plain pasta for my friend, too? No sauce or anything—in fact, the clumpier the better."

The waiter said he would see what he could do, and Parm beamed. *Maybe it won't be such a bad dinner after all*, Gladys thought.